Philip Stanhope Worsley

Poems and Translations

Philip Stanhope Worsley

Poems and Translations

ISBN/EAN: 9783337401269

Printed in Europe, USA, Canada, Australia, Japan

Cover: Foto ©Andreas Hilbeck / pixelio.de

More available books at **www.hansebooks.com**

POEMS AND TRANSLATIONS

BY

PHILIP STANHOPE WORSLEY

WILLIAM BLACKWOOD AND SONS
EDINBURGH AND LONDON
MDCCCLXIII

DEDICATION.

My dear Mrs White,

I hope you will pardon my wish to connect your name with the following poems. I can never forget that the perusal of them gave pleasure to your lamented husband,* and that he looked forward to their publication with that warm generosity of heart which led him to make the interests of a friend so completely his own. All who knew him, whether in his writings or by personal intercourse, will at once recall his genial wit and his liberal love of mankind; but it is to that sacred depth in his character, which you alone on earth could throughly penetrate, but of which many must have been aware, that my thoughts recur at this moment. In dedicating to you what I have written, to him I dedicate it whose spirit was and still is so indivisibly one with yours. I have no fear that you will reject any affectionate tribute to his memory, however slight and valueless in itself the offering may be.

Believe me, dear Mrs White,

Most sincerely yours,

P. S. Worsley.

Mrs James White, Bonchurch, I. W.

* Author of 'Eighteen Christian Centuries,' 'History of France,' &c. &c.

PREFACE.

THE following poems were nearly all written several years ago,* and evince, as I am well aware, much want of discipline and immaturity of power. It is my hope that kindly critics may, nevertheless, be able to detect in them the germ of something better, and that possibly with some readers they may have a permanent value of their own, if, as I have good reason to fear, my life should not be spared for future efforts. Of one thing I can feel assured, and that is, that I have resorted to no unworthy artifices in order to

* Many of them have already appeared in ' Blackwood's Magazine.'

veneer trite reflections, or to veil a dearth of imagination.

It may be thought by some that concerning the personal subjects treated of in one or two of these poems it were better to have meditated much than to have spoken freely. Since, however, there is a large class of readers, to whom compositions of this kind are probably in their way useful, and being unable, on a conscientious review, to discover anything morbid in their tone, I have thought even these pieces on the whole worthy of preservation.

The Translations will speak for themselves. They are faithful, and easily intelligible to all readers.

Of the Latin hymns here rendered into English, the originals will, with one exception (the 'Stabat Mater'), be found in Dean Trench's valuable compilation of 'Sacred Latin Poetry.'

CONTENTS.

POEMS.

PHAETHON.

NOBLE in presence, though a cloud of grief
Hung shadowy-dark upon his brows ; all else
Redundant with warm youth ; his radiant locks
Fair as a girl's, when stealing shades embrown
The wavy yellow, and the fine glint of gold,
Like fire-dust, sparkles in her sunlit hair ;
The while, from underneath his brooding brows,
Flashed eager expectation, mixed with pain
And wonder and delight—a surging sea,
Phaethon by the Sun's great portals stood.
There paused he, for a while incredulous
Of that huge architecture piled by gods ;

A

For such to earthly houses seemed that pile,
As field or forest, when a bird escapes,
To the one room which was his world.   But soon
He clomb the mighty threshold, and right on,
Through court, and vestibule, and shining hall,
And many a sweep of golden gallery,
Fared, as men walk an unfamiliar road
In dreams, not doubting—till he reached the King.

Him found he throned beneath a mimic sky
Cærulean, tricked with beaded adamant
For stars, and here and there ethereal steam
Curled into cloud, or what than snowy cloud
Is fairer of the ambrosial mists that move
In the god-haunted regions far from earth.
There, in mid choir, the orb of Artemis,
Lamp of the night, hung silvern, like that moon
Watched through her tears by a deserted maid
All night, who never tires of watching it,
But feigns a friendliness in that cold eye,
That only feeling heart in all the world.
Such and so beautiful in form and face,

Most lustrous of her starry satellites,
Shone the soft image of the lunar queen;
Who there and then had vanquished Phaethon
With passion, but that his enraptured eyes
Clung to the amber daïs, and to him
The sun-god, throned upon a lucent chair
Of ivory, compact with studs of gold,
Most wondrous; and beneath his raiment's hem
Peered a rich work of pearl and chrysolith,
Fit entertainment for the feet of gods.
But all how void and bare to him that sat
In night-imaginations, clothed with calm
Unutterable, through all his ample heart
Sated with office and the fiery cares
That haunted his day-labour! For, indeed,
Couched in those large and melancholy eyes,
Brooded an awful emphasis of rest,
That tranquil self-perfection, without pain,
Which, in their far-off musings, mortal men,
Though eloquently nurtured, find no name
Wherewith to name, not even in sacred verse.
So that, in sense and soul preoccupied

With state thus grand, the child of Clymene
Knew not, nor heeded if he knew, the Hours
Discoursing harp with harp celestial song;
Nor where the Seasons stood with lifted arms
Columnar to the broad blue canopy—
Spring flowery-zoned, and Summer wreathed with corn,
Autumn with vine-blood splashed from heel to thigh,
And Winter, bending over beard of snow.
So, ere he well returned into himself
From the weird influx of those dreamy orbs,
Went forth the voice of Phœbus :—" Phaethon,
Hither of mortal foot the first arrived,
Not strange, to no inhospitable halls
Thou comest; rather as a child comes back
From distant lands, this many a year desired.
Falsely he spake, who taught that Deity
Hath force to override a father's love.
I too have marked, 'mid yonder evil brood,
Dark under-questionings, and ill surmise,
Tamper in secret with thy name and mine.
Heard have these ears the open taunts of men,
Who brand me in their petty blasphemies

The forgèd pretext of thy mother's shame,
Bid thee go prove thy bright original.
Courage ! thou shalt not hence without a boon,
One that may well their slanderous tongues confound.
Thou from these realms demand whatever gift,
And I thy father will see justice done.
Spare not, but ask—I swear by ninefold Styx,
Dread oath, inviolable to gods and men."

Then leapt the heart of Phaethon for joy ;
For now before him, circumstantial, true,
Loomed the fulfilment of old phantasies
Nourished in early boyhood, on the banks
Of rivers or in bowery solitudes,
Whether by thought mapped out, or lighted on
Through lofty visitation felt in sleep ;
And readily he drew near unto his sire
And spake, appealing to that swerveless oath :

" My father, for thy words rhyme well with hope
Not questionless till now, if this be true,
And I thy child indeed, sprung from thy loins,

Shame were it to respond unroyally
To thy most royal prelude, and to ask
Aught facile or profanely pitched too low
For thy large heart and the reflected pomp
Whereof to-day I am called an inheritor.
That were an argument of craven blood,
Not worthy my great lineage. But do thou
Make me but once the splendid charioteer
Vicegerent of thy wain, the lamp of worlds ;
So shall my vast renown of embassage
Flash wide conviction both on gods and men,
And those false tongues put down eternally
Who vex the child of the Eternal Sun."

He ended ; but the brows of Phœbus lowered ;
And, stung with the anguish of a god, he spake :

" Child, thou hast asked a hard and perilous thing.
A thing to be denied even to Zeus.
Woe worth the moment when I swore by Styx
To this most dire completion of a will
So wayward ! Thou hast asked a boonless boon,

Not knowing that thou dost aspire to die,
Scared with a ruinous elemental roar
Too late, and sepulchred in floods of fire.
For who of mortal or immortal brood
May wield at will the horses of the Sun,
Not lightly tamed even by me their lord ?
O glean a little wisdom while thou mayest !
Is there not somewhere something to be found,
Sufficient to surpass this fatal boon ? "

So Phœbus ; but the child of Clymene
Stood firm, appealing to the swerveless oath ;
And all night long Apollo, with knit brows,
Heavy of soul and sore disquieted,
Through his wide palace wandered up and down ;
And, like the erring phantasm of a man
Slain traitorously and cast into the deep,
Who, for the dread want of a little earth,
Cannot find rest, so rest was none for him.
But the other, dreaming of the day's emprise,
Couched without care and in the bloom of sleep,
Lay till the early twilight, then rose up

Flushed for the boon, and found his glorious sire
Pacing beneath a pillared portico,
Still pausing when he passed the silver plains
Of two huge valves, embossed with graven gold,
Work of Hephæstus, and descript with all
Which earth and heaven and Nereid-haunted deep
Foster in wave or field or azure sky.
And ever as he paused he sighed, as if
Boding but little good to anything
In earth or heaven or Nereid-haunted deep.
Soon conscious of his child, he turned, and there
Urging divine dissuasion, half in tears,
Spake; but that other would not.   And they moved
Together, led by rosy-fingered Dawn,
In silence, till they reached the empyreal gates,
Which, to weird lutes receding, gave to view
Authentic heaven surpassing voice or dream.
For lo ! the awful chariot of the Sun
Flaring upon their front, itself a sun,
Wrought from metallic ores unutterable ;
And all the streaming surface intersown
With rainbow flames of keen-eyed jewellery,

And the long burnished axle thick with gold,

And wheels, a countless order, each like each,

Armed with a central star, and diamond-rimmed,

Blinding to men, save whom the gods keep whole.

For as with us plain earth is soiled and dull,

Matched with the marquetry of Indian kings,

So blurred and swarthy to celestial gems

Are earth-born ruby, pearl, or amethyst,

Opal, and tender sapphire, queen of stones.

Far up the vault a dazzling pavement, arched

Of diamond, chymic wonder, tracked with lines

Thrice-glistering, the diurnal route of wheels,

Scaled to the zenith ; and on either side

The myriad constellations sprang like flowers

Glassed in the cloudless hyaline.   Anon

Came forth that famous team caparisoned,

Four, and each fulminous with glancing flame,

Yet childlike each to the light-handed Hours

Who held him.   Twain about the golden pole,

Obsequious to long use, their station took,

And twain, with gleaming traces, in the van ;

And in a moment they were linked for speed.

But Phaethon stood silent—that white reach
Thwarting the blue serene, a belt of fire,
And all the flaming equipage unrolled,
In their essential lustre, form, and size,
So far transcended the pale counterfeit
Nursed in his dream : and once he half drew back
For terror ; nor the faint recoil escaped
The Sun-god, who made parley yet once more :

" Son, for thine hour is coming, not yet come,
Let for dear life a noble prudence trench
On blind unwisdom rushing to its doom.
Fly from this venture—for I know that Death
Will ride at thy right hand upon the car.
Yet, yet, take warning ; ask another boon."

He ended ; but the child of Clymene,
Through shame and curst ambition, stood to his quest.
And the god, condescending to his child,
Smeared face and hands and raiment with a chrism
Known to none else, most sovereign to repel
Tempestuous inroad of the fiery clime

Breathed by that fierce quaternion in the front,
And dashed in billowy flame from the echoing wheels :
Then, breathing on the brows, made all his mien
Godlike, severe, and large to look upon,
And placed the glittering reinage in his hands,
And helped him to his throne upon the car ;
But, ere he parted, spake a farewell word :

" Slack not the rein, nor from tense watch decline
Thine eyelids, lest thou find a doom not sought,
Maugre this fireproof chrism and godlike mien.
For know that underneath thee, where thou goest,
Swims earth, far-planted in the vacuous gulf,
Whose yawning interval both knees and brain
Sickens.   A league above this pontal arc,
Now seeming one with heaven, the dizzy sphere
Rolls a pernicious round, swarming with stars—
Bale overhead, and deep bale at thy feet.
In temperate self-distrust thy safety dwells.
Swerve not a hair lest thou abandon life.
Me heaven's revolving fabric all day long
Here in palatial splendour shall waft round,

Skirting the wide horizon, till I meet,
If the Fates will, thy duly westering wheels.
So night shall be divine indeed, while we
Slide with melodious music, unaware,
Back to these roseate realms, where men behold
Daily the soft sweet horizontal lights
Slow-deepening into spears of tender flame.
Farewell! may happy omens speed thy path!"

He ended; and the Hours with one accord
Stept sideways, and let go the willing steeds.

Then soberly and well did Phaethon
Hoard up and use that warning of the god,
"Slack not the rein, nor from tense watch decline
Thine eyelids"—so he watching slacked not rein,
But, from the godlike increase given to him,
Maintained an equal nerve, though sore afraid;
Nor even thus with all his power had curbed
That chivalry divine, but that the god
Infused a soul more governably mild
For that one voyage, making their defect

Somewhat incline, for easier vassalage,

To his son's lifted virtue. So he passed

Safe on his course, and all the heaven drank light,

And, touched with splendour, wine-dark ocean smiled,

Heaving with ships, black hull and snow-white sail :

And each land went to its accustomed work,

Of peace where peace, and war where there was war,

Nor omen of disaster rose at all,

Till, as he neared the blazing cope of noon,

Where the steeds flagged a little, as is their wont.

For steeper seems a hill just ere the bend—

Even at the point where Nature seems to pause

And listen while the sultry hour goes by—

Flat weariness ached through him, and he thought

How boonless were the boon if this were all ;

Nor did he cease repeating to himself,

" How worthless is the boon if this be all !

Broad is the way ; the steeds are tame enough."

Till, hungered with hot zeal, he seized the thong :

Then whirled it, curling it beneath the flank

Of the two vanward ; thence with sharp recoil

Crossing the arched necks of the hindmost two.

And lo ! the sudden insult dug like steel
Into the one heart of the fiery four.
They in a moment knew the vulgar hands
That held them, and their lordly eyes wept fire
For anger at the ungenerous pilotage ;
And each dilated nostril panted fire,
And the sides, heaving through their sleek expanse,
Stared with a noble horror, foaming fire ;
While, raving up the causeway, hoof and wheel,
With screams and anvil-thunder, a deafening din,
Rained earthward and to heaven a storm of fire.
So to the summit, from whose brows the team,
Thrice-maddening, prone adown the diamond arc
Swept, and a triple whirlwind of white fire,
Blown skyward, sloped upon the charioteer ;
Whom yet the chrism preserved invulnerable,
Nor even his eyelids faltered in white fire ;
But as a sick man stares, who, from some wound
Smit with red fever and delirious dream,
Thinks himself bound upon a wheel of fire,
Whirling, whirling for ever, and passes through
Cycles of anguish ere his eye can wink—

So, with like fascination, in the eyes
Of Phaethon was fixed a straining stare,
Yea, one to be remembered afterwards
By any that had seen it, man or god.
And though his brain shook, yet he could not wink;
And though his brain reeled, yet he could not fall.
Fixed were his feet, and o'er the ebbing reins
Drooped the spent fingers from the nerveless wrist,
Yet motionless and with no quivering drooped,
He standing like a statue of pale Fear;
While louder and more loud the affrighted stars
Cried from their burning vault, or seemed to cry,
Doom in his ears, and anger and fell revenge.

Then Ganges and a troop of Eastern streams
Fled backward, each one to his cradle cave;
Then the tall glaciers of the Polar Zone
Flushed crimson to the roots of their cold realm;
For all the fir-crowned Scandinavian hills
Night-shrouded half the months, tier over tier,
Blazed in the gloomy North, like beacon-bells
Lit for world-wasting Furies who bear down

In convoy, with wild omens of the end.
And all the peopled plains sent up a smoke
Of harvests reaped by fire, and flaming towns,
Till the hot clamour of those masterless wheels
Rang deadlier, mingled with the loud-voiced curse
Of men by myriads overcome with hell.
And a long cry came to the ears of Zeus,
Where in full conclave of the gods he sat ;
And, while he doubted, a great rainy heat
Fell slant and sudden on the Olympian walls,
And all the ceiling glared like molten gold,
And the rich cloisters like a forest glowed
Of resinous pines, with every trunk ablaze.
And Zeus and all the gods rose up together,
And saw the wide earth smoke, and the Sun's car,
Wrecked by false rule of ignominious hands,
Flare from the crystal zenith a long white flare.
And lo ! a change in the great Father's eye
Flashed darkly, and his face a moment writhed
With anger, as when taint of iron-rust
Writhes hideously a drinker's lips, anon
Whitened with cold inexorable wrath.

Mute stood the gods, while each in blank suspense
Stared on his fellow, wondering what should come.
He, turning to a sheaf of thunderbolts
Which lay there, piled for use, in the council-hall,
Chose one, thrice tempered, in itself a sheaf,
Needing no second to enforce the doom ;
Then leaning from his tower—" So perish all
Wild upstarts swoln with empire not their own "—
Shot once.   And Phaethon, caught in mid career,
And hurled from the Sun to utter sunlessness,
Like a flame-bearded comet, with ghastliest hiss,
Fell headlong in the amazed Eridanus,
Monarch of streams, who on the Italian fields
Let loose, and far beyond his flowery lips
Foam-white, ran ruinous to the Adrian deep.
And still the unbalanced chariot flared right on,
Till, from the main line swerving, the vast heap
Fenceless, and falling a stupendous fall,
Horses and chariot, in the Western Sea
Plunged, and the rushing shower of that fell hiss,
Heard ghastlier than a myriad-throated storm

B

Of Pythons strangled in their noisome lair,
Seemed to drink up with lips the shuddering world.

   Scarce had the sound expired, ere gods and men
Heard wonderingly a beat of iron wings ;
For Darkness, with a beat of iron wings,
Vaunting herself sole mistress of the world,
Sprang from that watery pyre ; and heaven grew
     black
Before her, and man's earth, being breathed upon,
Smouldered in silence till the fires died out.
Dark was that night and long, as is the length
Of two nights and a summer day between ;
And all the while men saw not with their eyes
The face of wife or child or friend or foe,
And all the while men spake not each to each.
But as a captive, in some gloom-bound cell
Under the level of a stormy lake,
Feels that the roof has shifted and the walls,
And, where he finds himself, there crouches down
Mute, and in horror lest his blood's quick beat
Rive up the ruin and let in the lake—

So, with clenched hands, they, crouching whisperless,
Feared lest a heart-vibration should unbind
Loud dooms that rocked in ambush overhead.

Meanwhile Apollo, through that dire eclipse,
Dwelt in the dim light of his azure halls,
Likest in beauty to the perfect form
Stamped on the soul of some great statuary
Waking and sleeping, who with touch divine
Breathes life and love into the chill dead stone,
And warms it with the warmth of his own soul ;
Till some one finds him in the cold grey dawn
Laid mute by the mute marble, his long toil
Just ended, and the mighty brain at rest.
Like to that dream which made the dreamer die,
So proud, so beautiful in pensive pain,
Sat Phœbus, veiled in dark divinity,
Dreadly repentant, as a god repents,
Nor yet so wholly wrapt in self-remorse,
But that at times his gloomy reins would feel
Wild frenzies, ruminant of wrong to Zeus,
Zeus saviour of the world by that one stroke.

But loss is loss, though worlds be profited,
And deep love will remember, there and here.

But when the long dread night was overpast,
Came to Eridanus, the lord of streams,
Clymene, and the weeping Heliades ;
And Phaethon they found, or what seemed he,
There, with his eyes in ashes, and the once
So radiant locks by cruel thunder scathed,
Recumbent in the reeds, a charred black mass,
Furrowed with trenchant fire from head to foot.
Whom yet with reverent hands they lifted up,
And bare him to the bank, and washed the limbs
In vain ; and, for the burnt shreds clinging to him,
Robed the cold form in raiment shining white.
Then on the river-marge they scooped a grave,
And laid him in the dank earth far apart,
Near to none else ; for so the dead lie down,
Whom Zeus, the Thunderer, hath cut off by fire.
And on the tomb they poured forth wine and oil,
And sacrificed much substance thirty days.
Nor failed they to record in distich due

How from a kingly venture kingly fall
Resulted, and a higher than human fame.
And there, amid those comely services,
Brake into song the weeping Heliades :

"O that much sighing could these lips restore,
And make them bloom with kisses as before !
But Phaethon returns no more, no more !"

And answer made the childless Clymene :

"O that this love, which on thy welfare fed,
Could with new pangs renew that lovely head !
My Phaethon, my child, is dead, is dead !"

And yet again the weeping Heliades :

"O to be guided to that sunless shore,
There clasp the glimmering phantom o'er and o'er !
Since Phaethon returns no more, no more !"

And once more sang the childless Clymene :

"O if to that dark land I might be led,

Loose his dear life, and leave mine own instead !
My Phaethon, my child, is dead, is dead !"

So ever sang the weeping Heliades,
And so made answer childless Clymene.
Cycnus the while, half brother and whole friend,
Sat housed in lamentation far apart,
Brooding alone, discomfited with ills.
He oft in the night season, chill with stars,
Sat moaning in the thickets, and by day
Sat moaning in the thickets, till his voice,
By reason of long sorrow, conceived a key
Sweeter than any harp : and tales grew rife
Of him that sang so sweetly.   Dream in peace ;
Yea, waste thyself long while in tender song,
Cycnus ;—the bending woods listen for love,
And old Eridanus flows faint with sound.
But ah me ! for thou singest in vain, in vain !
Heart-cold is Persephassa, and her ear
Cold, and impenetrable by plaintive song ;
Cold is the dust of thy familiar friend ;
All, save thine own deep heart, for ever cold !

NARCISSUS.

LIKE as some solitary woodland flower,
Far out of reach, upon a perilous ledge,
Flaunts its rich colours in a maiden's eyes,
And seems more fair because desired in vain,—
So he, a stream-god's son, more beautiful
Than all his peers, serene and passionless,
Lived whole of heart, in scornful self-delight
Vacant for ever. Love, that comes to all,
Sought not nor found him. Many raving words,
The multiplied despair of aching hearts,
Thickened around him, and he heeded not ;
Ay, though enamoured Echo, woodland nymph,
Pursuing him with love, filled the deep air,
The caves, and the bleak rocks, valleys and hills,
With murmurs meaningless to none save him,
Wasting away till she became a voice,

Vague, incorporeal.—And thus it went,
Till one who also loved him all in vain
Uttered this dying curse :—" So let him love
A fiery love, and, loving, not enjoy !"

And the suns travelled till there came a day,
When, heated from the chase and tired with toil,
Whether of chance, or by some envious Fate
Misguided, he bore on with flagging steps
Unto a pure cold fount, where never bird
Nor mountain-goat frequented, clothed around
With fresh green turf, and secret from the sun.
Thither no devious track of mortal feet
Led through the shady labyrinth of wood ;
No sound of shepherds, calling from the bowers
With melody of flute or vocal play,
Made welcome for the weary flocks at noon ;
Only the immemorial silences
Kept haunt for ever on those flowery floors,
Where the sweet summers ever came and went,
And went and came, and even from the bees
Year after year their customary spoil

Concealed, as in a secret treasure-house.
And there, in evil hour slaking his thirst,
He in his spirit conceived a thirst tenfold,
Which water could not quench. For, as he drank,
Leaning to the cold lymph, he saw therein
The phantom of himself clear as the life,
The mirrored white and red upon his cheek,
The loose locks clustering round his snowy neck,
Full of divinest beauty—saw and loved.

O Love! thou art the theme of many songs;
And some have thought thee but a froward boy,
Risking thy random arrows here and there,
Careless who suffer from thy pastime wild:
Some paint thee pensive and serene of mood,
Gentle, with very heaven upon thy face,
Planting the deadly nightshade at the heart,
Whereof men die, and leave wild words behind.
And melancholy music strange to hear.
But whether thou wert born in Rhodope,
And sharp winds sang around thy couch of snow,
And thy young heart grew hard among the hills—

Or, cradled in the warmth of tropic isles,
The softnesses of life corrupted thee,
Till, to wear out the languid summer hours,
Thou couldst not but be cruel to mankind—
Or whencesoever or of whom thou art—
Herein thou wast supremely merciless,
That the twin shafts, whose piercing should create
A mutual sympathy in different hearts,
Thou without pity at one single breast
Didst aim too surely, so that wild desire
Tended to no sweet haven, but must rave
In desolate unrest without a home !

Ah ! there and then hot hope, with eager eye,
Sprung from that first fierce hunger in his blood,
Flashed change upon his face, and o'er his soul
Rolled moments like to years.   Ah ! then and there
Were passionate strivings with extended arms
To fold a shadow ; and he sought not rest
Nor food ; the hours went on ; and still he lay.
Gazing upon the form that answered him
With silent gestures, silent moving lips,

Seeming to mean a not unequal love,

Till the truth dawned upon him, and he knew

Himself alone of all to his own heart

Was cruel—for himself was his own love,

Himself his own despair.   Then in his ear

Sudden there spake, or seemed to speak, a voice :

" Life without love, or with a love unreaped,

Makes every hour a death ; but death comes once.

Better to die, for death will make an end."

Then spake he, weaving his own funeral dirge,

Accents whose wildness might unnerve the rage

Of wolves that wander in the Hercynian glens,

Roll back the rivers from their seaward march,

And rive compassion from the core of rocks :

" O forests, dreaming of the years of old,

Ask of your branches, whether green or sere,

Whether by night or day, in calm, in storm,

They may remember any love like mine.

O Love, dread Love, I know thee—but too late :

Come, feast thine eyes ; thou art indeed avenged !"

And lovelorn Echo, startling at the cry,

Paused in her bower a moment, then took up
The shrill-toned sorrow, and from hill to hill
Tossed it in mocking mood, until the voice
Failed in the far-off clouds—Avenged! Avenged!

So when the Sun unyoked his flaming steeds,
And through the glimmering silence, calm and slow,
The dark world drifted to the bourne of sleep,
Came the death-angel in the cool of eve,
Who seals impermeable to life and light
The charm-constrainèd orbs, and solemnly
O'er the lost lover bending in the gloom,
Touched the pale brow with ceremonial wand.
Whence a sad wonderment, the pain of dreams,
Hung round his trancèd spirit like a mist;
And all about him snatches of old songs,
Heard in old hours among the Oréades,
Mixed with a meaning never felt before,
Floated—dark legends of mysterious love
Unhappy, and of hope for ever fallen,
Fallen for ever, like his own—and still
Haunted him more than all a simple strain

Sung by Liriopé, the naïad-nymph,

His mother, how a maiden golden-haired,

Trusting to treachery and led by love,

Followed a stranger from her father's halls :

' She like a rose just opening into bloom,

' Which one hath paused in passing to admire,

' Anon hath gathered, and against his heart

' Worn for a little hour, then cast away

' For ever, and remembers it no more ;

' But all the while it lieth where it fell,

' Silently drooping on an alien earth,

' Alone, unpitied of the passers-by ;

' Nor any more availeth that the showers

' Strive with sweet influences to lend it life,

' And golden suns caress it as of old ;

' Nor to have been in native loveliness

' First among flowers availeth any more,

' So lowly doth it lie, so far hath fallen '—

Here Echo seemed to answer—Fallen ! Fallen !

Slowly and sad, like one that hath her wish,

And finds it other than she hoped, not gain,

But bitterest loss—which when the dying heard,

The pulses of his heart grew faint and still,
The life-stream halted and then ebbed away;
From limb to limb crept the damp languor cold;
And he lay silent in a seeming sleep,
Moveless like marble, with unlighted eyes
Changelessly fastened on the crystal pool,
And countenance snow-cold, which even in death
Bore impress of unutterable desire.

Then, after twilight, the stars one by one
Peered from the broad blue curtain of the heavens,
And the blanched delicate features of the dead
Showed whiter in the broken misty light.
There he lay all night long, until the birds
Sang in the mirthful morning, and the sun,
Piercing a slant path through the woven green,
Rested upon a flower, ambrosial, sweet,
Alone in grace among the forest flowers;
And therein lay embalmed the love, the life,
Of that bright being, who but yesterday
Was Beauty's youngest-born upon the earth.

VERSUS AMOR.

CHANGED love forsooth in me you fear.
Go to :—no whited tale I ask,
No mocking ineffectual mask ;
The coarse plain truth shall serve us here.
All sin forgive save loss of gold ;
This cursèd creed hath priests of old ;
For this my love is counted cold.

When first I saw thee face to face,
That careless summer years ago,
Why never whispered friend or foe
One warning of this dire disgrace ?
Weak wish !—few words the sequel tell :
My pomp of outward fortune fell ;
Yet this could I sustain, and well.

Constant to minister in pain,
True woman would have loved me more.
This reckless hollow dream is o'er;
I kneel to no false star again.
Yes, recreant slave, take back thy vow;
Earth's choicest crown about thy brow
Were bribe too mean to tempt me now.

For suffering, that doth make men wise,
Came thunder-like, and shook my sleep.
I rose; I bought experience cheap.
God sent the gift of open eyes.
I thank Him thou art not my wife,
To load the lagging years with strife,
To damn me in my dream of life.

Henceforth I neither love nor hate;
Thou art a thing forgotten, dead.
This painful arrow, swiftly sped,
Hath saved my soul ere yet too late.
Let him who seeks thy spouse to be
Fetter the winds and reap the sea,
But hope not love from thine or thee.

I curse not now thy lust of pelf—
Thou, in thy dearth of pure desire
Selling thy very heart for hire,
Art curse sufficient to thyself.
Guilt's secret stab shall find thee yet,
Though not this sin thy conscience fret,
Though me thy narrow soul forget.

And never hug thyself in this
Blind hope of impotent revenge,
That I, too sick to care for change,
Shall feed despair with buried bliss.
Not so—a larger heart than thine
Shall to one music blend with mine
In love thou never canst divine.

Once and for aye thy toils are torn ;
I am not thine to slay or spare.
From far-off fields of wider air
Thee and thy selfish peers I scorn.
Go, vilely reap thy share of earth ;
I yet believe in woman's worth,
Where deeper love hath holier birth.

Farewell, without a farewell kiss ;

I leave thee here alone with crime.

Yet, for the sake of olden time,

I would that I could teach thee this :

Search the wide world, and thou shalt find

No penury of baser kind

Than this thou hoardest in thy mind.

STRONG AS DEATH.

Go thou hence, and make her
    Thine for evermore ;
Bind my cherished day-dream
    To thy home and heart.
Thou hast health and riches ;
    I am sick and poor ;
Yet I would say something—
    Listen, ere we part.

In the morning twilight,
    In the stillness deep,
When they say that visions
    Speak with tongue divine,
I from long night-watchings
    Fallen into sleep,

Dreaming on my pillow,
  Saw thy love and mine.

She with bended eyelids,
  Sad, yet passing sweet,
Came in angel aspect,
  White and like a star—
White, save where the life-pulse
  Slowly toward her feet
Fed with secret streamings
  One long crimson bar.

If thine after-hardness,
  If thy love grown dim,
Paled that face of sorrows,
  Wrung that bleeding heart,
Well may Nature wipe thee
  From the world's great hymn :
'Twere a shame so burning
  That the stones would start.

Treat her with affection
  Lest thou hear of me,

Lest a quick pursuer
   Sailing in thy wake,
Lest a dark avenger
   On thy summer sea,
Armed with indignation,
   Smite thee for her sake.

Feed not the delusion
   That dead men forget ;
Surely I shall see thee,
   Know thee, and come down ;
If thou cause her sorrow
   Thou shalt pay the debt,
While thick-woven curses
   Clasp thee like a crown.

Cursed when thou wakest,
   Cursed in thy sleep,
Cursed in the day-time,
   Cursed in the night ;
So thy life shall languish
   In corrosion deep,

Till the death-fiend call thee
And thy soul take flight.

* * * *

God ! what maddening fury
  Drives my dragon breast,
While the dark dread shadows
  Thicken round my room,
While the faint lip quivers
  Ere the last cold rest,
Thus to hint of cursings
  On my couch of doom !

How can dreams discredit
  One whom God made true,
Write a man disloyal
  Who can feel and love ?
'Twas an envious anger
  Burned me through and through.
While I seemed to hearken
  Voices from above.

Ah ! this fire within me
　　Spake I know not what—
Stand a little nearer—
　　Bathe my dying brow—
Be the doubt I fastened
　　On thy faith forgot,
And the love remembered
　　Which would warn thee now !

Thou this friendly warning
　　Take in friendly part,
Nor, when I sleep silent,
　　Let the word go by—
Not alone unkindness
　　Rends a woman's heart ;
Oft through subtler piercings
　　Wives and mothers die.

Though the cord of silver
　　Never feel a strain,
Though the golden language
　　Cease not where ye dwell,

Yet remaineth something
  Which, with its own pain,
Breaks the finer bosom
  Whence true love doth well.

If the ends be diverse
  For the which ye live,
If, while she yearns ever
  To the far away,
Thou thy coarser feelings
  To the world dost give,
And with labour heapest
  Treasures which decay—

This would plant sore trouble
  In that breast now clear,
And with meaning shadows
  Mar that sun-bright face.
See that no earth-poison
  To thy soul come near!
Watch! for like a serpent
  Glides that heart-disgrace.

      *   *   *   *

Hark ! the wind loud-sweeping
   Bears a voice I know ;
Hark ! it calls my spirit
   To a land of gloom.
As that storm sinks dying,
   Life's lamp waxes low ;
Ere that storm is ended,
   I must meet my doom.

Shall there fall true sorrow
   On my timeless grave ?
False or true, what matter,
   Since the Lord is just !
Mercy, not men's mourning,
   Hath the power to save,
When the wheel is broken,
   And when dust is dust.

O this life how pleasant,
   To be loved and love !
Yet, should love's hope wither,
   Then to die were well,

Steeled with trust that something
   Will be given above,
More than lost remembrance
   Of our earthly hell.

Kneel, thou blest of heaven,
   While I yet draw breath ;
Pray we once together
   For thy virgin flower—
Once before thy marriage,
   Once before my death—
Kneel, for very quickly
   Strikes the iron hour.

I can pray with pureness
   For her welfare now,
Since the yearning waters
   Bravely were pent in.
God—He saw me cover
   With a careless brow
Signs that might have told her
   Of the work within.

Ask to be found worthy
　　Of God's choicest gift,
Not by wealth made reckless,
　　Nor by want unkind ;
Since on thee dependeth
　　That no secret rift
Mar the deep life-music
　　Of her guileless mind.

Then let this toiled spirit
　　Pass to the Most High,
Clothed in ghostly silence,
　　Out of human ken !
Be our farewell finished,
　　Leave me here to die,
In the selfsame moment
　　That I breathe " Amen !"

　　*　　　*　　　*　　　*

Is the wind not fallen ?
　　Doth my brain yet burn ?

Is he gone for ever ?
    Am I quite alone ?
Whose is that dire presence
    Passing by so stern ?
Comes the King of Terrors
    Thus to claim his own ?

What ! this dark destroyer
    Comes not as we dream—
In my brain a furnace,
    In my bones fierce fire !
While the heart, tormented
    With the refluent stream,
Fails in pain, help, Father,
    Ere thy child expire !

Keep these flickering senses
    Self-contained and clear,
Which, when life shone sweetest,
    Passion's whirl defied.
Take these phantom-voices
    From my dying ear,

Voices of the bridegroom,
   Voices of the bride !

If I love too dearly
   One who lives below,
Yet I never wholly
   Razed thee from my breast.
Lead me, scared and shaken,
   From this house of woe :
Hide me, Lord, and heal me
   In some bourne of rest !

When my youth was younger
   That is now grown sere,
Thou didst fence with pity
   One who knew thee not :
In my last wild anguish
   Shall thine ear not hear ?
Shall thine eye glance heedless
   Over this one spot ?

Who is this that bendeth
   O'er my bed so pale,

Such as I have seen him
　　In some painting old?
O let no more spectres
　　That sweet aspect veil—
Lift me, gentle Shepherd,
　　Bear me to thy fold!

Yes, the vague earth-passions
　　Feed a grander love,
And the soul expandeth
　　Ere the life's last beat—
Yes, the conflict endeth;
　　There is help above—
Though to die was bitter,
　　Yet is dying sweet!

WISDOM.

Who loveth wisdom loveth life ;
   Who finds her finds a hidden pearl.
Far from the roll of vulgar strife,
   The tumult and the whirl,
A cloudy pillar is her throne.
Mingling with all things, yet alone,
Queenlike she watches from the towers of Time,
Clothed in an immortality sublime.

Her empire is above, below ;
   Her eyelids slumber not nor sleep ;
Through life's wide systems breathe and grow
   Her musings high and deep,
And ever deeper, ever higher.
Her words are like a lamp of fire

Sowing with light dim worlds that none hath sown,
Searching the silence of the dark unknown.

Her spirit is not bent to earth ;
　　Not hers to dream the hours away ;
Seeing the secret of her birth
　　She learneth how to pray;
Her mind is in an even health,
Constant in sorrow, meek in wealth ;
Her lips are never raised against the truth :
She holds in reverence both age and youth.

She dares not lend herself to wrong.
　　Though slow to blame and mild of mood,
Sharp are the arrows of her tongue
　　When crime must be withstood.
Yet pride and wrath are not for her ;
Ruling by mercy, not by fear ;
Supreme, yet judging not another's sin,
She slayeth not the sinner but would win.

Form of sound words she loveth well,
　　Words that the listening spirit reach,

Conversing now in parable
  And now in children's speech.
She works regardful of the end ;
She cleaveth to a faithful Friend,
In whom she moveth toward eternal rest ;
In whose great name she blesseth and is blest.

PROGRESS.

THE broad advances of material power,
The onward sweep of intellectual good,
And nations moving into manhood new
Through wisdom and authentic civil change—
O soul-expansive creed ! O faith to stir
The individual breast with hopes divine,
And breathe forgetfulness of private wrong !
But when I asked myself what these have done,
What failed to do, I felt as if an air,
Steady and chill, from some waste wilderness,
Swept cold across the chambers of my heart.
For through the heavy multitudinous roll,
Heard underneath the noises of the hour
From Life's dark hollows, as I thought, a cry
Unheeded, inarticulate, went up,
Which forcibly found words within my breast :—

Still we suffer wrongs untold,

    Robbed of peace and joy and health,

Slowly slain, both young and old,

    For the rich man's greed of wealth.

How long shall our hearths lie cold ?

How long shall our lives be sold ?

Rise, ye men of nobler mould,

    Say it shall not be for ever !

Vainly doth the poor man groan,

    Vainly doth he speak his grief.

"Work on, till thy days be flown ;

    Seek not, save in death, relief !"

It is thus they mock his moan,

While they take from him his own,

Leaving him the grave alone,

    Where to sleep at rest for ever !

Shall there not deep vengeance fall

    On the tyrants pitiless,

Holding cursed festival

    In a people's heaviness ?

Vengeance late or soon will fall
On the oppressors one and all,
Covering, like a funeral-pall,
These iniquities for ever !

O would that all men who have eyes to see,
Who feel the earthquake heaving in its chains,
Would lay to heart the remedy of things
Disjointed, ere they perish, and would turn
Where lies the one hope of the groaning earth !
Nor will I doubt my country shall find help—
Not in the selfishness of social war,
State agitations, and the building up
A Babel of unripe democracies ;
But in the charity of man to man ;
In the acknowledgment of common blood
Drawn from a common Father ; in the sense
Of Christ's desert wherein we all are rich,
And of our own wherein we all are poor.
This is that touch of nature which will make
The whole world kin, and bring " the golden year."
And God be thanked that many to this end

Are working, by the unfaithful and inert

Derided, not defeated, and, though faint,

Pursuing; the laborious pioneers

Who point the scope of elemental Right,

Who make the rough ways smooth, the crooked straight,

Who lift the valleys even with the hills,

And on a secret anvil, hour by hour,

Unforge the fetters of Humanity!

STRENGTH.

In strength there ever dwells of right
  Some quality of noble name,
Which through base uses keeps alight
  A remnant of celestial flame,
And cannot leave him wholly vile
  Within whose breast it takes abode,
Since this one spot, this little isle,
  Must still retain the stamp of God.
In him who, not of kings the heir,
  Carves out a crown by kingly work,
Must needs be that some virtue rare,
  Some godlike moral grace, doth lurk.
This, shining forth, shall colour lend
  To wrong, or questionable act,

Till the world dreams a righteous end
Where only sophists can defend,
   And Faith becomes the slave of Fact.
Yet is it an effeminate thing,
   A woman-weakness, still to crave
For works that make the world to ring,
Or setting up some idol-king
   For violence pronounce him brave.
For stronger far, and in their strength
   More honourably due to fame,
Are they who through the stormy length
   Of combat kept a flawless name ;
Who, reddened to the brows with strife,
   Have nourished hearts not cruel still ;
Men who, though widely taking life,
   Shed blood for conscience' sake, not will :
Who sheathed the sword when peace might be,
   And, bravely glad, confessed it gain ;
In whose severe sublimity
   Envy detects no fatal stain ;
Men of a perfect mould ; and such,
   Who knew themselves and knew their time,

We cannot honour over-much
  In story or in rhyme.

Strong is the statesman who can wield
  A nation to his single will,
Teach its blind passions how to yield.
  And lordly destinies fulfil ;
Who to one point, whate'er befal,
  Makes every shapely purpose bend,
Becoming all things unto all,
  So he may gain an end.
Yet greater oft is ill success—
  Later in time they reap applause
Whom factions could not ban nor bless :
  Found brave enough to lose a cause ;
Who, 'mid a grovelling race and prone,
  Walked honestly erect and proud,
Who dared not lie to gain a throne,
  Nor struck their colours to the crowd.
Such shall not lack renown, till when
  Cometh an iron age at last,

Sneering at all that makes us men,

    Cursed with contemnings of the Past ;

Who, reaping where they have not sown,

    Wax selfish in their base degree ;

Who think the breath they breathe their own,

    And slur the light by which they see.

This is the noblest strength to seek,

    And fadeless still the crown remains,

Which once He wore who, strongly weak,

    On Calvary was wrung with pains.

To suffer, and without complaint,

    Makes grandeur more divine than all ;

This to high places lifts the faint ;

    This is the hero's coronal.

To wither in a dark disgrace

    Which half a word might wipe away,

And clothed with calumny to face

    Contempt and hatred day by day,

Because the half-word that would change

    Our destiny were best unsaid—

O wide and elevated range
    Of hearts to worthy interests wed !
So blest the fame-regardless thought,
    Which, to divine attractions true,
Feels that the life which hath been taught
    To suffer hath been taught to do !

Who once hath chosen the ranks of right,
　　With clenched resolve by his choice to stand,
Saves a people oft in their own despite,
　　And loveth wisely his native land.

He bears a praying heart in the strife,
　　Sworn knight and true of the Christian cross,
Against all evil wars to the knife,
　　And is firm of faith, though he suffer loss.

Better tenfold take any defeat,
　　Than rise to success by a doubtful deed,
Or craven-like, after the risk and heat,
　　Gather safe laurels where others bleed.

He doth not count his coffers his own,
  Nor teach his children to scrape and save,
No living worker dares to disown,
  Nor brands on his brother the name of slave.

He cannot conform to the worldling's part.
  Never despairs of a righteous cause,
Stands up for God's poor with hand and heart,
  And scorns to defend unequal laws.

Yet cares not to court a death sublime
  For poets in distant years to sing,
But bravely, in God's own place and time,
  Yields up his life without questioning.

Never say that good is waning,
　Virtue falling from the van ;
Nor, in saddened strains complaining,
　Preach the thanklessness of man.

If some profitless self-seeker
　Win much praise and public gold,
Not for this thy work be weaker,
　Not for this thy courage cold.

Whoso in life's task hath taken
　Glory for a worthy goal,
Hath for a light dream forsaken
　True magnificence of soul.

Think it then nor shame nor pity
    That no crowds applaud thy name ;
Strive on—save the leaguered city,
    Though another reap the fame.

If thy prowess hath not found thee
    Meed of honour in the state,
Think of many a martyr round thee
    Daily doing something great.

So thy people reap the harvest,
    Little recks who cast the seed ;
Guerdon, high as thou deservest,
    Dwells in thy own holy deed.

EDITH.

REARED among woods and waters from her birth,
Fatherless long ago, an only child,
Edith, the shrine of many memories,
Far in the country with her mother dwelt—
Her mother known ensample of true worth,
And cast in olden type of virtue rare,
A kind good woman, something stern withal,
Of courtesy beseeming one whose mind,
Warped into gentleness by force of will,
And ruled by inward ordinance severe,
Moves to its end deliberately just.
But Edith ever was a happy child,
Roaming about in wild light-heartedness
Free as a silver-footed waterfall,
Which down the bosom of a sun-lit crag
From ledge to ledge, with many a whitening curve,

Leaps in a luminous ecstasy of life,

Hurrying on weariless in a vain pursuit

For ever, and for ever vanishing

Gulfed in the shingly sands that far beneath

Spread smooth, and shining with the ocean-dew.

And her bright form, touched with all delicate grace,

Among her playmates on a summer eve,

With a peculiar music of its own,

Held the will captive, and enchained the eye,

That once a hard man seeing her made pause,

Led by a quiet instinct unforeseen

And self-responsive to some secret chord,

To wander into old remembrances,

Dead dreams, and scenic shadows of the mind,

Till, in that breathing-time of tenderest thought,

Silent he lapsed, nor wholly without tears,

Into a genuine blessing and a prayer

That far and few might be the days which found

Sorrow and her inhabiting one home.

Not unfamiliar from her childhood up

Were the old legends of the land to her,

And the rude poetry of rustic hearths,

And visionary tales of Fairyland.

Reinless imagination day by day

Learned to cull sweetness from whatever flowers

Haunted the range of her sequestered life ;

So that two lives within her seemed to dwell,

One nurtured in the semblances of things,

One amid abstract phantasies afar,

Both happy, each receding into each.

O Edith, would thy face had been less fair,

So had thy fate been fairer! For when she

Was budding into gentle womanhood,

Fresh from her eighteenth birthday, kept at home

In overflow of simple merriment,

With a few guests, her friends of equal age,

There came a handsome stranger to the place,

Skilled in all suasive accents, dark and tall,

Who saw, and set his mark upon the house.

Virtue is more than omens, and herself

Is prophet to herself, and still the law

Is changeless which hath said " The equal suns
Alike upon the evil and the good
Shine, and the sweet rains without favour fall "—
For a more large humanity than ours
In nature's soul, with a more even pulse,
Dwells, though one life and though another cease—
Else surely had some angel, Argus-eyed,
To whom is given to read like open scroll
Black thoughts that fester in the hearts of men,
Sent forth some wonder to unfold the crime.
But now, as ever, the wide face of things,
Slowly dissolved, is drawn into the dark ;
Slowly the muffling mist, as heretofore,
Climbs from the valley, and leads up the night
Even to that shelving slope, whereon was built
The ivied cottage, of those two the home,
There growing from the basement to the roof
Till the slow-creeping vapour indistinct
Hung like a funeral shroud upon the place.
Ah ! yet a little while, and the great Sun,
From his deep harbours moving outward-bound.
Smites the dominion of the Night with sails

And the long flashings of his gilded oars !

But who may utter warning, who may know,

How soon another darkness shall come up,

And press like iron on the ruined brows

Of one who seemed too beautiful to die,

And force her shuddering to a land far off,

And cold, where the sad billows never feel

Day with his shining sails and gilded oars,

A land of darknesses unutterable,

Whence neither feet nor wings nor strength nor tears

Conquer a passage to the realms of light ?

O Edith, Edith, whither then shall fly

That laughter of the heart, that fresh delight,

Which brooded o'er thy being, and could change,

After the varying impulse of thy mind,

Reality into a pleasing dream,

Or dream into a sweet reality ?

Meanwhile the tale that hath been often told,

And yet so often must be told again,

From small beginnings, wilfully incurred,

Hourly was working to the fatal end.

First came the bow in passing, and anon

The casual greeting when she went abroad,

And then the chance companionship, which soon

Grew into stolen interview, and now

For the first time and for a stranger's sake,

Who lightly smiled her scruple to the winds,

She kept a secret from her other heart;

And the pre-sentient questionings within,

That should have saved her, learned to reason down

With soulless shallow plausibilities,

Even to the last believed against belief,

Till from that blind perversity there sprung

The Atè of an edgeless intellect,

And her vain lightness, self-beguiled to fall,

Fostered a strong delusion, that a lie

Came in the semblance of eternal truth,

And one disloyal in all thought and act

Seemed admirable, and made discourse of love

So nobly, that she thought him half a god,

And knew him not, nor ever wished to know,

Urging soft flatteries, and smooth-lipped guile,

And seeking to abuse her virgin ear
With perilous words, that to forbidden dreams
Familiarize and mould the unwary mind.
So for five moons he laid perpetual siege
To citadel that thought not of defence,
Till on occasion cunningly contrived
He made himself possessed of that, which once
Discarded, woman hath no more to lose ;
Then hasted from the ruin he had wrought,
Yet, with a hideous fraud in his farewell,
Vowing return ere many days to claim
Her hand, and take her for his wedded wife.

And the days rose and set, and he came not—
But there came gifts of money ; and her heart
Would ask her, had she sold herself for this ?
No, 'twas a wicked doubt, it could not be,
How dared she cast such slur upon his truth ?
He would return, he would not let her die—
But still she felt ashamed to touch the gold ;
And the fierce canker like a fire did eat
Her soul, and shook the roses from her cheeks,

And in her eyes the melancholy light
Did plant of pensive hope, that will not die,
But leads a dying life beyond its hour;
And made her but the ghost of what she was;
Till her companions laughingly would say,
"Edith is pale and thin; she is in love."
And then her lips would smile a negative—
A sad cold smile, at variance with the heart.

Once on a winter's day, beside the fire,
Waking from gloomy reverie, she saw
A sudden whiteness in her mother's face,
And knew the stony horror of her eyes
Interpreting the change of form, now grown
Discernible, and reading all at once
The fatal first dishonour of the house.
Then weeping she knelt down, and uttered all,
With sobs and passionate heavings of the heart.
As one who cannot loathe herself enough.
When lifting up the shame of guilty brows,
Half-dead with desolation, she beheld
A gracious countenance bent over her,

And falling tears that mingled with her own
From eyelids eloquent with comfortings
Undreamed of, and a kindness large as heaven ;
And wonder rushed upon her, when she knew
The force and fulness of a mother's love,
And how we starve it with indifference,
And cast it out to wander in the cold,
And to its ceaseless knockings all the night
Close the dull ear and selfish heart, yet still
It feeds upon itself in solitude,
And for the dear one hopeth golden years,
Content to be rejected and love on—
O God, the riches that we spurn to use !—
And her knees smote together, and she swooned.

As when a heartless child for self-delight
Hath stolen a little nestling from the nest,
And loves it with a cruel careless love,
And promises to hoard it for his own,
Till in the sunset, growing tired of play,
He casts it from him as a worthless thing,
And leaves it cowering on the naked earth,

Bruised on the breast, and cold, and all alone—
But in the twilight comes the mother-bird
And brings it food, and strives to make it eat,
And with such shelter as the place provides
Fences it from the night that cometh on ;
But all in vain—for never shall she hear
That voice among the voices of the bowers,
Never behold the little wings outspread
Drinking new vigour from the vernal suns—
Like to that bird, in such a lonely doom,
Lay Edith, tended by a mother's love ;
Nor only in one sorrow ; for she thought,
" Ah ! never so my child that shall be born !
He cannot rest in any mother's arms ;
None can he find to mould his baby lips
Into that name, as a familiar thing.
Kind Heaven ! how sadly in the after-time
Shall he hear others, happier than himself,
Praise feelingly and well, with earnest eyes,
Tear-glistening, dim, that love beyond all love,
A mother's, and shall wonder what they mean !
How often, in some hour denied to sleep,

Heavy with darkening cares, shall he look forth
And speak his anguish in the night's dull ear,
That cannot hearken what he has to say,
And find no succour left in the cold earth,
No succour in the cold stars overhead !
Or if it be a daughter that I bear,
Child of my shame, O God, she may be like
Her mother, and may sin as I have sinned,
But not like me to find an early grave ;—
So shall my name sound hateful in her ears,
And I shall feel the curses of my child
Who never knew me, whom I never knew,
Raining in fire upon my prison-house
Eternally." Forthwith her eyes grew wild
With terror, and she shrieked, " I have done with
        hope,
Despairs have fallen upon me, and I die !"
But there were ministering lips which gave
The medicine of comfortable words,
Saying, " I will not leave thee nor forsake.
But if the hour might come, which cannot come,
When even I thy mother could forget,

Lives there not One who will remember still ?"
And in sweet consonance with gentle lips
Tender caresses, given by gentle hands,
Were sadly trifling with her golden hair;
And the mute movement uttered more than speech.

From that day forth she passed not out of doors,
But with her mother stayed alone at home,
Craving continually, both night and day,
Pardon and mercy from offended Heaven.
And so she wore herself with utter grief,
Feeding for ever on a broken heart,
Even until her travail-time came on.

*   *   *   *   *

Seven slow hours, from noon into the night,
While the red fire upon the hearth burned slow,
And fitfully, without, the gusty winds
Blew the rain westward, slanting on the panes—
Seven slow hours she watched her daughter's couch,
Who lay there with still brows and features still,

Set as in sorrow, white, and worn, and cold,
Dreamily dying, having borne a child—
Seven slow hours she watched, but in the eighth
Sad orphanhood was on the new-born life.

As one who, torn with sickness and slow pain.
Lies whisperless with horror all night long,
And ever in the ghostly flicker of light
Quails with a doubtful death-stare in his eyes ;
But when the shivering wind blows chill with dawn,
And the grey stealth of twilight with pale feet
Treads on the listless hills, or half in fear
Feels tremblingly about the dark ravine,
While the lone eagle from her sunless rock,
Veiled in the wet smoke of the rushing streams,
Stirs through the cold a hollow cry far off—
Sad Echo wails—that moment the sick man
Feels the tense nerves relaxing, and the brain
Showered on by sweetness of Elysian dews ;
Then marble-mute, with the white-breasted smile
Of simple childhood wreathing his wan lips,
Lies stirless in the murmurings of the morn,

And stirless in the golden afternoon,
Till, when the sun's red splendour sinks at eve,
He, fresh from dream of flowers and resonant rills,
Opens wide eyes rejoicing, saved by sleep—
As life's rich tumult seemeth sweet to him,
Thus in her dying sweet was death to her,
To Edith, when she passed from the cold earth.

And now the mother of the dead rose up
With mien of fire, and from her flashing eyes
Shot curses—so might Clytæmnestra look,
Nerving her heart up for the devilish deed.
But all the while in softer shades revealed,
Under the workings of tumultuous wrath,
Loomed, mixed with wrath, the mighty mother-heart
Of Rachel, who of old in Ramah wept
Her children, by an evil doom cut off,
And would not any more be comforted,
Since these, her only comfort, were no more.

She rose, she gazed her last upon the dead,
That mother, frenzy-fired with grief and pain,

Then, full of a wild anger half-divine,
Uttered her soul in meanings like to these :

"O Earth, O Heaven, if aught in earth or heaven
Can feel, if judgment may exist at all,
How can ye longer witness what men do,
And not be shaken to the core with pangs
Unutterable, nor furiously consume
The demon-lives that work you violence?
That which I feared with an exceeding fear
Hath surely come to pass, and I remain,
Whelmed yet alive, amid a burning wreck
Of ruin, scarcely comprehending all,
But only that I am not in a dream—
O God, that I could make myself unborn!
That altogether taken from a world
Which never seems to have been made for man,
But for a habitation of the fiends,
So foul it is, so wasted with revolt,
I might find somewhere sleep, or, if not sleep,
Utter extinction, which were best of all;
Since to me, girded with so dire a curse,

That from which Nature doth recoil and shrink
Has come to be a thing desirable,
Foremost of blessings, and the goal of hope.

"God help me, but I will not weep to-night !
Is this an hour for unavailing tears,
Sighs, and the listless folding of the hands,
When I have lost her who was all my hope,
My heart, my darling flower, my one delight ?
I childless henceforth, and without a joy,
Must live my lonely remnant of dark days ;
The light shall rise for others, not for me,
Mine is the dewless desert black with gloom,
Mine the long bitterness of death in life,
Mine the slow sunless hours for evermore ;
I will not weep, lest I forget revenge !

"Would God my child thou hadst not perished thus !
For thee Death came not timely as a friend,
Nor with kind rest as to the weary sick,
Nor pure, as when he cometh on the young,
Nor painless, as he visiteth the old ;

But, ere thy summer rose, a cruel man
Laid wait to snare thy unsuspecting love,
Thy heedless early love, and for vile lust
Fed like a frost upon thy budding life,
A heartless enemy, whom God endow
Here and hereafter with his changeless curse!

"Ha! I have sworn to teach thy babe to pray;
And thus will I fulfil my plighted oath,
As righteous reason justifieth aloud.
Yes, I will teach thy lisping little one
To name his father in his daily prayers,
But not for blessing.   From his early years
His tender unimprinted waxen heart
Shall take the fearful mould of filial hate.
God may not hear me, but He will the child.
Those orphan hands uplifted shall have power,
More than an outraged mother's cry, which yet
Surely shall not return unto me void,
To clothe blood-guiltiness with fiery flame,
And brand the brow with damning characters
Which each one that beholds shall read, until

From the destroyer and his hated house
Love like the yellow leafage falls away.

"Surely, O Vengeance, thou wilt prove my friend :
Not now, but sometime in the far-off years ;
It may be at the merry banquet-board,
Or when his children throng him round with smiles,
Or when deep-housed amid the calm of night
In his wife's arms he dreams that all is well ;
O then appear to him, in such an hour,
Then fix thy fangs in his uneasy soul,
And plant there a consuming misery,
A dire remorse at enmity with sleep,
A sensible strange madness of the mind,
Musing alone, impregnable to hope,
A wearing, wasting leprosy of heart,
Never to pass away, though he pray much
For peace, sweet peace that is so far to find,
Until by utter anguish beaten down
He hide his head in an unholy grave
And slake his hot thirst in the nethermost hell.

" Ay me ! I would not weep, I would not weep '

Child, look not upward from thy couch so cold,

With such mysterious meaning in thy face,

Such awful sorrow lingering on thy lips,

Such strange reproaches in thy sightless eyes.

Thy words come back—I cannot bear their sound.

Better in dead oblivion once for all

To lie down senseless in the senseless earth,

Than that the plaint of thy departing speech

Haunt me for ever, ringing in my ears,

With power to make me weep against my will.

' O God, O God, thy mercies break my heart

For sorrow.   I have not been merciful

To thee.   I pierced Thee to the soul with sin ;

And with strange agonies from hour to hour,

Made all thine aching wounds to bleed afresh.

Yet, Father, even so take back thy child

Washed white with the pure blood that cleanseth all.'

So spake that voice which never shall speak more.

Then to me turning :—' Mother, once again,

Yet once ; the sound is sweet to dying ears ;

Say thou forgivest me ;' and I replied—

F

' God hath forgiven thee, and I forgive
Even from the heart '—and then her thin white lips
Said, as I think, ' Forgive *him*.'—It is well—
She died her death, and dying she forgave—
Aye, it is well—but what have *I* to do
With mercy or forgiveness any more ?

" O, I will walk abroad and cry to heaven,
Disturber of men's peace, till whoso hears
In the dead hours the unfamiliar shriek
Far-off, shall shiver on his couch for fear ;
Then haply some one, meeting in the way
My ghostlike form, shall ask me, ' Who art thou,
Who with thy crying dost coerce the Night,
That would be deaf but cannot—such a voice
Of wild despair, rending her rest, goes up ? '
And then will I unfold the heinous wrong—
Or if the sullen darkness fail to hear,
I will go forth and wander up and down,
Seen like a spectre in the haunts of men,
White-haired, and silent with a fixèd eye,

Till my heart-agonies unsealed become
Audible, though a load is on the lips,
And the dread rumour bruited in the land
Keep his head slumberless, and turn to fire
The air he breathes, and make his senses fire!

" Yet better might it be that I should nerve
My feeble friendless arm, and move with stealth
From place to place, and rest not day or night
Crouching with hungry hope in wait for life,
Till fierce revenge and unoblivious hate,
Yoked to a mighty purpose, had worked out
Full reparation. Surely this were well—
Afterwards let me die—my life for his!

" Merciful God, my soul is dark as death!
I am not what I was; about me hangs
A cloud, all blood, which maketh red like blood
All things that I behold; and fearful shapes
Beckon me onward unto fearful deeds—
Are these thy angels? often heretofore

Have I knelt night and day and prayed for love.
Shall I kneel now and pray for deathless hate,
Hate that shall never swerve, never repent?

" My soul is dark—I know not what I would.
Can murder wipe out murder? O my God,
Who helpest them to right that suffer wrong,
Plead thou my cause or even slay me here.
I swoon in darkness; let me feel Thy hand;
Make haste; uplift me; bear me to the light;
O clasp me closer; let me cling to Thee,
Cling to Thee only, who alone art left;
Thee who alone canst any more appease
The maddening fire that burns into my brain—
Hearken, O God, my God, forsake me not."

So cried she an exceeding bitter cry,
And, falling forward, sank upon her knees
And wept before her Maker. When she rose
A change had passed upon her—for she stood
Silent like stone, and seemed from head to foot
Clothed in a settled anguish. Lip and brow

Were many a winter older ; and her hair
Was changed ; but on the soul was written peace,
Or that which slowly ripens into peace.

So cried she an exceeding bitter cry—
Would that thy ear could hear it, and thy heart,
Thou treacherous spoiler, who hast done this thing,
And hadst no pity in thy brutish breast,
No feeling, no remorse, no human pang !
Therefore against thee, in the scroll of God,
Stern things are written for the wrath to come.
Blood, like a witness crying for thy life,
Ever smokes up to the discerning Heaven,
Big with the vapour of an iron rain,
Heavy to overwhelm ; since never yet
Hath risen, nor shall rise while earth remains,
More damning testimony against a man
Than is the voice of her who weeps a child,
Slain by some hater of the light, like thee.
Wherefore repent, if thou canst yet repent,
Nor hope be all too late.   Surely thy doom
Drew closer round thee from the moment when

She whom thy crime half maddened into crime
Left thee amenable to God alone.
Ah wretch ! who shall divorce thy load of thought ?
Who lend thee any ward or subterfuge ?
What charm defend thee from thy harrowing dreams ?
What priest or prophet shield thee from thyself ?
Go, seek a watchword while it may be found,
A watchword to unlock the guarded gates,
One that when spoken from the heart's deep heart
Makes placable the armèd Seraphim,
Who sentinel with brows of frowning fire
Fields unpolluted by the steps of guilt,
That they may hear thee, moaning bitterly,
And look with pity on thy asking eyes,
And stoop and pluck thee from the throat of hell,
And set thee safely in the fold, before
Heaven thunder, and amid the roll of wrath
Thine agony's strong voice in vain climb up.

ERINNYS.

Ὅστις δ' ἀλιτὼν ὥσπερ ὅδ' ἀνὴρ
χεῖρας φονίας ἐπικρύπτει
μάρτυρες ὀρθαὶ τοῖσι θανοῦσιν
παραγιγνόμεναι πράκτορες αἵματος
αὐτῷ τελέως ἐφάνημεν.

Though stark it lieth and cold in clay,

Though it utters neither good nor ill,

There is that which my dagger could not kill—

A haunting horror night and day,

That makes my blood stand still—

That makes my spirit shrink and shiver,

That dwells within me for ever and ever,

A dark and terrible dream, wherewith I cannot away !

Nightly and daily I die with fear,

Lest the breeze, as it wanders far and near,

Should speak my story in mortal ear ;

Or the Hand that writes in letters of fire,
When the raving clouds contend in heaven,
Should flash my name in the wild far-gleaming levin,
And the pattering rain should conspire,
With ever-heedful tones, as it fell,
This bloody rumour that cries from hell,
Slowly to shape and syllable.

Suddenly in a frenzied fright,
With cold damp brow, and stiffened hair,
And lips that trembled in vain for a prayer,
I started from my bed,
In the deep heart of the silent night—
For there grew in the dark a lurid light,
And my eyes were chained to a ghastly sight,
The white weird face of the dead;
And I saw the blood of the red wound drip,
And the wasted finger laid on the lip—
O for darkness of eyes, darkness of mind!
Great God, let the heat of thine anger strike me blind!

The very breath I breathe is a secret strife,
And might well make a coward of the brave.

I shudder to see the light of life ;

But death with a hundred hells is rife,

And I dare not lift the poison or knife,

And suddenly seek the grave.

There is rest for all, but not for me ;

I discern not any term or scope,

But a ghastly hope, which is not a hope,

For an end which is never to be.

And still the Angel claims the price of guilt ;

Still the Voice haunts me through the weary years,

Full of anguish, full of fears,

Seeming to search the distant spheres,

And to whisper the tale in a thousand ears,

How the crimson river of life was spilt.

And in the desert gloom of my breast

So long this fiery curse I bear,

That to me now, in my mad despair,

Change of pain would be almost as sweet as rest !

THE SEARCH.

TRACKING each inlet
  Painfully well,
Lonely she wanders
  Down in the dell;
There, while the night-winds bleak
Whiten her wasted cheek,
Something she seems to seek,
In the pale starlight,
  Down in the dell.

And there is one who
  Knows very well
Why she walks nightly
  Down in the dell—
Knows where the maid, unseen,
Weeps like a Magdalene,
And what the searchings mean.

In the pale starlight,
  Down in the dell.

Covered up somewhere,
  He knoweth well,
Lies a rich treasure
  Down in the dell ;
She to and fro doth flit,
Thinking to find it yet
Where he hath hidden it,
Under the alders,
  Down in the dell.

Cold is the starlight,
  He knoweth well,
Chill sweep the night-winds
  Down in the dell—
Ten times more chill and cold
That which her arms would fold
Rests underneath the mould,
By the dank alders,
  Down in the dell.

Seemeth too surely
Something not well,
Where blow the night-winds
Down in the dell :
He, who in cradle deep
Laid there a babe to sleep,
Never once paused to weep,
Where the leaves whisper,
Down in the dell.

Hollow-eyed dreamer,
God guard thee well
From the dread secret
Down in the dell !
Better in wildered brain
Feed a false hope in vain,
Than by its father slain
Find thy lost darling
Down in the dell !

THE MEETING.

Bitter was the tale I dreaded,
    Grief of heart for evermore,
When, from years of weary travel,
    Landing on my native shore,
I sought out the ancient village
    And the well-remembered door.

Long it was since any tidings
    Reached me wandering o'er the wave,
And my soul for certain knowledge,
    Though it held a curse, did crave—
Though the melancholy answer
    Only echoed of the grave.

I had left three little children
    In the years of long ago—

But past joy is present sorrow ;
　　Painfully the seasons flow—
Who am I to be delivered
　　From the broken hopes below ?

I had left an angel woman
　　Guardian of the tender three—
Is she dead or is she living ?
　　Is her spirit true to me ?
Well I know that many winters
　　Cannot change her constancy.

And I sought the well-loved cottage,
　　Skirted by the poplar tall ;
Waited by the garden-wicket,
　　Listening to the waterfall ;
And I caught the pleasant odour
　　Of the jasmine on the wall.

Then I entered, and she knew me,
　　And sank fainting in my arms,

On her face I saw imprinted
Midnight watchings, pain, alarms.
And her children clustered round me,
Undivided, free from harms.

MUSIC.

What means this siege of ravished heart and brain?
What may these spiritual echoes bring to mind?
It seems not wholly joy nor wholly pain;
But each with each inhabiteth one strain,
Till thence a marvellous ecstasy combined
Makes sorrow not unwilling, tears pure gain.
Is it a yearning memory of bliss
From some far life that knew me long ago,
More painless and more equable than this,
Ere yet, fast-bound with iron gyves within,
I died into this prison-house of woe?
Ah! that I yet might find some useful lore,
Not wholly deadened by the clasp of sin,
To conquer that delightful land once more!

THE CHARGE.

In ferrum flammasque ruunt.

'To the charge ! to the charge !" and there lingered
    not one ;
But the deepening thunder of hoofs cometh on,
And the iron earth reels underneath ; they are gone—
    Stern were the faces that flashed for an instant past.
      Onward, onward they go,
      Angels of ruin and woe,
      Right to the heart of the foe,
        Sure as a sea, fierce as a blast.

On they sweep, in the storm of their fiery zeal,
Where the deep lines await them with cannon and steel,
Closing round them, as billows that close round a keel—
    Horsemen six hundred but now passed sword in
    hand ;

Passed, but return not again—
Only a struggle and strain—
Then from the wounded and slain
   Rides a thin remnant, a scatterling band !

MILTON.

God gave to thee the keys of heaven and hell,
With power to bring their sacred things to light.
His hands upbore thee in thy fiery flight.
He who inspired the seers of Israel
Fashioned thy tongue to speak the unspeakable ;
So that for ever with the sons of men
Thy sacred sentences shall deeply dwell,
Graven and grafted with an iron pen,
As of a ruler by the might of mind.
As Zion standeth with her crown of hills,
So thou, above Earth's storms and wasting wind,
Art crowned of God.   His is the thought that fills
Thy utterance.   His own breath thy being doth move.
I tremble and bow down—I feel and love.

STANZAS TO WORDSWORTH.

LIKE solitary branch of oak or elm,
Torn off in early summer, when the year
Was greenest, orphaned in the forest-realm,
The whispered by-word of each sylvan peer ;
Which all despairingly some few days' length,
While the sap dwindles to a scantiest tear,
Feeds a dead life with its inherent strength—

Too soon, alas ! the brittle blackening leaves
Shrivel their veiny network, once so fair ;
No more that lost bough pleasant tune receives.
But harsh and hollow, from the idling air ;
And nerves once quick to pleasure and to pain
Wholly forget the sunlight's fostering care,
Wholly the sweet dews and the mellowing rain—

Such did I fondly deem myself, but thou
Hast taught me with new forms to over-write
That fatal old imperious blank, and now
Find I companionship as wide as light,
True sympathetic rapture, which distils
There on the spirit's most harmonious height
Rich revelations from the stars and hills.

There that good Faculty doth build her nest,
A refuge from self-waste, and hourly reaps
Wholesome vicissitude and boon unrest
In other haunts than where the gross world sleeps ;
Whence she discerns that Earth's dumb-seeming sphere
Heaves warm with pulses from its deepest deeps,
And mighty voices large with love doth rear.

Each wind, its own majestic cadence pouring,
Wanders articulate the realms of air ;
In the great zone of waters, hushed or warring,
Lives language that no centuries outwear ;
And, with peculiar poesies endued,
Each hour can answer speculations rare
With master-meanings culled in solitude.

This thou hast taught me, this art teaching still.
My new-found nature quaffs the piercing rain
Shed from thee, and is moulded at thy will
To read high matter in a simple strain.
Thrice blest who owned thee early for their seer,
Who, finding thy sweet fountains not in vain,
Preached the remedial virtue far and near!

Well said the Greek that universal earth
Buries the brave, and is their monument;
But death to thee hath been an ampler birth,
Whereby thy being with mankind is blent.
Graved on men's hearts thine epitaph lasts long.
Now are those hard lips learning to repent,
Who scorned thee once, the Nazarene of song.

Even when we wept, a little while ago,
Unfaithful, that thy place knew thee no more,
The mental essence, moving to and fro,
Flashed in our eyes thy renovated lore,
And filled all corners with instinctive truth.
He errs who tells us that thy life is o'er,
Nor reads all round him thine eternal youth.

Therefore to thee whose bones God's call await
In that fair earth whereof thy poet-power
The lapsed significance did intimate,
And clothe each herb and individual flower
With music and thine own life's noblest part,
I, a weak proselyte, love's simple dower
Offer not worthless from a poor man's heart—

Yea, thanks and love for that serener code
Which, in a safe and stormless avenue,
Teaches the humble to interpret God,
Which even by exaltation can subdue,
Chasten, and thrill with light those evil dreams
Which made life's heavier meaning seem the true,
And change this desert to a land of streams.

O to what height advanced were we, now low,
Could we but once inform with that great light
Our tyrant strengthlessness—the ebb and flow
Of objectless desire—yea, boldly smite
Custom, that old usurper, who doth draw
All nations in his net by lordly right,
Not by true service and kind wisdom's law !

We fail ; but thou, alike in youth and age,
Calm-browed with patience, like a Phidiac god,
Satst loftily withdrawn from vulgar rage,
Not faithless, though thy fellows left untrod
Stairs of thy building.—O large heart and brave,
Stars are thy raiment, not this lowly sod.
Gazing on heaven I gaze upon thy grave !

DOMINE, QUO VADIS?*

THERE stands in the old Appian Way,
  Two miles without the Roman wall,
A little ancient church, and grey :
  Long may it moulder not, nor fall !
There hangs a legend on the name
One reverential thought may claim.

'Tis written of that fiery time,
  When all the angered evil powers
Leagued against Christ for wrath and crime,
  How Peter left the accursèd towers,
Passing from out the guilty street,
And shook the red dust from his feet.

* See Mrs Jameson's 'Sacred and Legendary Art,' p. 180.

Sole pilgrim else in that lone road,
    Suddenly he was 'ware of one
Who toiled beneath a weary load,
    Bareheaded in the beating sun,
Pale with long watches, and forespent
With harm and evil accident.

Under a cross His weak limbs bow.
    Scarcely His sinking strength avails.
A crown of thorns is on His brow,
    And in His hands the print of nails.
So friendless and alone in shame,
One like the Man of Sorrows came.

Read in her eyes who gave thee birth,
    That loving, tender, sad rebuke;
Then learn no mother on this earth,
    How dear soever, shaped a look
So sweet, so sad, so pure as now
Came from beneath that holy brow.

And deeply Peter's heart it pierced;
    Once had he seen that look before;

And even now, as at the first,
　It touched, it smote him to the core.
Bowing his head, no word save three
He spake—" Quo vadis, Domine ? "

Then, as he looked up from the ground,
　His Saviour made him answer due—
" My son, to Rome I go thorn-crowned,
　There to be crucified anew ;
Since he to whom I gave my sheep
Leaves them for other men to keep."

Then the saint's eyes grew dim with tears.
　He knelt his Master's feet to kiss—
" I vexed my heart with faithless fears ;
　Pardon thy servant, Lord, for this."
Then rising up—but none was there—
No voice, no sound, in earth or air.

Straightway his footsteps he retraced,
　As one who hath a work to do.
Back through the gates he passed with haste,
　Silent, alone, and full in view ;

And lay forsaken, save of One,
In dungeon deep ere set of sun.

Then he, who once, apart from ill,
    Nor taught the depth of human tears,
Girded himself and walked at will,
    As one rejoicing in the years,
Girded of others, scorned and slain,
Passed heavenward through the gates of pain.

If any bear a heart within,
    Well may these walls be more than stone,
And breathe of peace and pardoned sin
    To him who grieveth all alone.
Return, faint heart, and strive thy strife;
Fight, conquer, grasp the crown of life.

DE PROFUNDIS.

As when a bark, bereft of oars and helm,
  Slopes on a savage realm,
And the lone sailor all against him finds
  Sky, shore, and waves, and winds,
So drift I helpless, and bear far and wide
  God's anger at my side.

The magnet-star, that should have won my will,
  Shone through me, sweet and still,
When the world-billows, in their golden play,
  Lured me with smiles away—
Thus went I forth, and wasted life and name
  Laboriously, with shame.

Often the barren rocks with lifted voice
  Cried sorrow on my choice ;

Often the faithless sands about my feet
    Told me my self-deceit ;
The winds sang warnings, and each hollow shell
    Breathed in my ears a knell.

So I that wandered the wide seas for gain,
    And left the poor in pain,
Now for sweet health in a voluptuous air
    Find plentiful despair,
And from soft dreams of an Elysian land
    Strike on this iron strand.

Fierce from long sleep the sins of summer roll
    Their anguish on my soul ;
They seize me in their arms, they wring with shocks
    My heart out on the rocks.
Men gaze—none reckoneth in his heart-belief
    How holy a thing is grief.

O vision of a maiden pure as snow,
    I love thee well, but go !
Go—for sweet joy may not be yoked with shame,
    Our bourne is not the same.

Harps in the pure sky measure thy low prayer ;
    Mine falls I know not where.

Tell me, dear friends, if one with bleeding feet
    Stand where the sea-waves meet
The bending sky—one pale, with anguish marred.
    Doth he with wan regard
Seem to yearn hitherward, and feel and know
    This my contempt and woe ?

Cold is my heart, mine eyes are waxen dim,
    But could I once find Him,
And lave with tears his thin feet crimson-wet,
    There were good hope e'en yet.
But ah ! he tarrieth with his virgin-trains,
    Not caring for my pains.   .

Would he not gather up these drifting spars,
    And with new bolts and bars
Heal the crazed wreck, and make her strengthless knees
    Fit to re-stem the seas ?
But oh ! far hence on lilied couch he sleeps,
    Not dreaming of the deeps.

Would he not steer me in my broken bark
    On through the lurid dark?
Then, though the red storm veil him, I might hear
    His voice, and feel him near.
Thou fool!—yea, something like to this might be
    For others, not for thee.

Say, can the chill lips that in death lie mute
    Breathe music in the flute?
Or, in the dark earth coffined, the dull ear
    Unseal itself, and hear?
Then canst thou also not in vain arise,
    And labour, and be wise.

How merciless in front, how black with gloom
    Frowns the sought goal of doom!
And if I look behind me, rolling dire
    Curl the long waves in fire.
O Thou far-listening, if thou hear my cry,
    Come quickly, for I die!

SNOWDROPS.

WITHOUT the dry trees groan and shiver,
  The curtained sun in his cloud doth sleep,
And through the chamber-casement ever
  Murmurs the roll of the distant deep.

By the maiden's side on the couch were lying,
  Blending their delicate green and white,
Children of winter, half-closed and dying,
  Flowers that are born ere spring is in sight.

Slowly she spake in a voice of sorrow :
  " Gentle flowers, live yet to-day,
But when I shall have died to-morrow,
  Droop ye, and wither, and fall away.

" Yet a few hours, then droop and wither ;
　　Silently fade and fall with me ;
Far from the sun we will rest together,
　　Shut from the sound of the moaning sea."

Ah, poor maid ! nor father nor mother
　　Soothe thy spirit passing away ;
Only my hands, the hands of a brother,
　　Gathered those snowdrops yesterday.

Why wilt thou take the heart I cherished ?
　　Rightly, O Death, art thou called unkind—
Victims twain by this stroke have perished.
　　One in body—and one in mind.

SPRING.

Lo ! once again the leaves, the flowers,

In grassy glades, in tangled bowers,

Rejoicing in the vernal hours,

Rejoicing in the sun and showers,

   Call on us to rejoice,

To pause and gaze where all doth seem

More beautiful than in a dream ;

Sweet is the hill, the wood, the stream,

   And sweet is every voice.

O flowers, O leaves, why bloom ye here ?

Ye should be yellow, dry, and sere—

O Death, lift up thine icy spear,

And smite the splendours of the year ;

   I cannot bear them now !

Joys which reviving suns impart
Lie heavy on a breaking heart ;
Wild are the arrowy pains they dart
Into an orphan brow !

WEARY is the life I lead,
  Beating air with vain endeavour ;
Love is left to weep, to bleed ;
  Those dear eyes are closed for ever !
  Closed for ever and for ever !
Not again shall I behold thee,
Not again these arms enfold thee !
  Thou art gone for ever !

Nothing now is left for mirth ;
  All my dreams were false and hollow ;
Thou, alas ! hast left the earth ;
  May it soon be mine to follow !
  Mine to pass the veil and follow !
Eyes of olden hours shall meet me,
Lips of olden love shall greet me,
  In the day I follow.

METHOUGHT I heard thy gliding footstep near;
But this was my delusion, the mere dream
Of fever; and things are not as they seem.
Life hath a wild confusion, a sore pain
Of wonder whirleth in my heart and brain;
And all I know is that thou art not here.

Seemed that a low voice in my hearing spake:
" I fold thee in my arms; my heart is thine!
We that were sundered meet; thy heart is mine!"
In the sweet trance my breast hath ceased to bleed.
And my lips whisper, Thou art here indeed—
Vain word, that left me wailing for her sake!

So, when I saw that I was mocked in mind,
I went forth quickly, to beguile my pain.
Thou soft air, breathe upon my burning brain.

Clear the dark mist that on my soul doth press !
But oh ! my thoughts were far and fathomless,
And not to be swept off by summer wind.

O were it not enough that some grand blow
Fall heavy on our lives, and blot the sun,
Sear up the heart, and leave us once undone,
But each light hour that passes on the wing
Turns to behold, and planteth a new sting,
And stirs with fire the torpor of our woe !

In the bright world to live alone, alone ;
This is the change : I feared it, and I feel.
Were it not better that one death should heal,
One black rain, falling from the iron sky,
Out-rival the divine machinery
Moving within, and turn my heart to stone !

NIGHT.

MOTHER of mysteries, immortal Night,
Of old the monarchs of the world might quail
What time thy seers unfolded to the light
Things in the womb of Time, a wondrous tale,
When burning words writ on thy starry veil
The doom of waning empires could impart.
O the long labour and sad watchings pale,
The deep devotion and expense of heart,
Wherewith they builded up their high Chaldæan art !

But thou art grander in the latter days.
Though the old worship is for ever past,
And Heaven claims other nobler forms of praise,
Thy sacrifice is pure, thy rites shall last,
Who now with thoughts unutterably vast

Feedest the careful climbing intellect,
Proving Creation's towers how deeply cast,
And Love's pervading law strong to protect
The wandering worlds that sail the eternities un-
    wrecked.

Thee silence with a potent influence dim
Enfoldeth, a celestial energy;
Silence, old Nature's noblest choral hymn;
Silence, the treasure-house of meanings high ;
Rich with all hope ; the world's great armoury.
Strokes on her soundless anvil fall like snow ;
Yet mouldeth she bright bolts of Phantasy
To flash divinity on things below,
And perfecteth with care brave Reason toiling slow.

Day hath its sanctity and proper grace,
And peace is in the twilight's healing hour.
Yet hath my day oft worn an iron face,
And stolen away the speech of leaf and flower.
Often the setting suns forget their power.
Then have I sought, nor ever failed to find,

Some hidden far nook in the night's deep bower,
Stamped with the tone and temper of my mind,
Where I might weave me charms which grief could
    not unbind.

Wherefore have men polluted thee with crime,
Thou that dost seem too pure for earthly stain ?
Wherefore at this devout and holy time
Doth the foul spirit of the deed of Cain
Walk to and fro where peace and love should
    reign ?
Wherefore do men delight to imitate
The darkness that is in thee, and not deign
To learn the lesson of thy starry state,
And strive for very shame to tear themselves from
    hate ?

NIGHT.

O THE beautiful strange visions seen within the silent
 night,
Then when heavy eyelids weigh on heavy eyes that
 hate the light,
When the careworn spirit, resting from the penance
 and the pain,
Sees in dreams long-vanished Edens rich with love and
 life again !

Then dark thoughts no more molest us : dull and
 leaden-hearted men,
Cruel in their lust of riches, make not breath seem
 bitter then.
Doubt casts not its poisonous shadow. Slow despairs,
 that rankle deep,
Pass away, as if for ever, exiled from the land of sleep.

Then once more we see the faces that are laid beneath
  the mould ;
Then we hear sweet meaning voices—voices that we
  loved of old ;
Then the stainless life returneth laughing through the
  merry hours
On the ancient paths of childhood, sown around with
  starry flowers.

Who would lose the dear illusion—who would wish
  to feel it less,
Though it make the radiant morning thick with blight
  and barrenness ?
Let the weary waking hours, forlorn of hope, creep
  slowly on,
So on slumber's couch we borrow joyaunce from the
  summers gone.

O Sleep, dear to all, then dearest when strong sorrow
  bows us down,
Charming care with golden hours, and smoothing out
  the furrowed frown ;

Thou that blottest from existence half the fever and
the fear—
Come, kind minister of healing, come, for thou art
needed here.

Come, as yesternight thou camest. I had deemed that
nevermore,
Save to grief, my darkened spirit should unlock its
sealèd door;
For within my breast I shuddered, shadowing forth
the things unseen,
And the Past, save in its sorrow, seemed as it had
never been.

For I thought on wasted life—I saw a future fearful
hour,
Dread misgivings, formless terrors, evil sights of evil
power,
When the clock ticks slow, the minutes linger in their
sullen flight,
And the ghastly day's oppression is but trebled in the
night.

When no more the shattered senses round the throne
   of reason dwell,
Thinking every sight a spectre, every sound a passing
   bell ;
When the mortal desolation falleth on the soul like
   rain,
And the wild hell-phantoms dance and revel in the
   burning brain.

Now the months and years of old, far from the outer
   feud and strife,
Lay before me like a picture breathing with the breath
   of life ;
And I saw my early home, as when it was a home to
   me,
In a happy land, and fairer than bright lands beyond
   the sea.

There it stood — the self-same village -- even as in
   hours of old,
When the stately sun descending dipt the dazzling
   panes in gold ;

And methought for many an hour, yea many a peace-
ful day and night,
All that space of earth was steeped in one delicious
faery light.

And I marvelled not, though round me clustering life
and beauty grew
In the paradisal stillness visited by forms I
knew ;
Yet there were, beyond all others, features that I loved
to trace—
Ah ! too truly I remember—for it was my mother's
face.

'Twas no wonder that I knew thee, as thy kind eyes
turned to mine,
Happy in my happiness, while I was thinking not of
thine ;
And I heard thy silver accents sweeter than all music
flow—
Ah me, but the lapse of summers changes many things
below !

"Mother, we will dwell together evermore," I seemed
    to say,
"Far from hence life's wheels are whirling; scarce an
    echo comes this way.
Here an uneventful rest shall fold us in a dream of
    peace,
Here our love through silent seasons grow with infinite
    increase."

But I woke—as one who, coming from far lands be-
    yond the wave,
Finds not any face of welcome—all he loved are in the
    grave.
Scarce the ancient house remaineth, bartered for a
    stranger's gold ;
Foreign fires upon the hearth, whose very flame is
    deathly cold !

Surely 'twas some evil angel woke me ere the dawn
    began—
Fiend, who could have heart to break the slumbers of
    a wretched man !

Time enough grief's drooping banners once more to
behold unfurled,
When the warm imperial sunlight widens through a
weeping world !

Breathing soon a finer sorrow, I, who had not wept for
years,
As I pondered on the vision felt my eyes grow dim
with tears ;
And I know that never, never, while Time wings his
weary flight,
From my heart of hearts shall perish the remembrance
of that night.

God be thanked that thy sweet phantom swept across
my dreary way,
Lighting up thine own dear footprints lest thy child
should turn astray.
Now for me, like loving sisters, Hope and Memory
embrace,
Each alike henceforward living in the sunshine of thy
face.

I

Let me pass in some sweet vision of the seasons long
    gone by !

Some stray touch of dreamy fancy haunt me slumber-
    ing ere I die !

Kindred hands of welcome lead me to the country far
    away,

Where the spirit never needeth interchange of Night
    and Day !

HADES.

Cowper, thy lines of tenderness so deep
Pierce home, and many times have made me weep.
In heart those darling lineaments I see,
And feel that I am like yet unlike thee ;
Like in my loss ; unlike, because in vain
I seek an outward charm to soften pain,
And in the wide world nevermore can find
Fit semblance of the form which haunts my mind,
Nor aught presenting visibly and well
The consecrated Past wherein I dwell.
Deluding fancies, even while they gleam,
Melt like the faery frostwork of a dream.
Hark, the familiar footsteps round me fall !
See, a still shadow moves along the wall !
Low murmurs in the air, more felt than heard,
Linger prophetic of some wished-for word.

'Tis a vain instinct both of eye and ear.
Fond dreamer, cease—thou hast no mother here.

My father, I remember to this day,
And shall remember till I pass away,
How, on an evening, in a happier time—
And, I half think, in some more blessed clime—
In the dim silence thou didst turn to me,
Not worthy of my mother nor of thee,
And, with a manly tear upon thy cheek,
Of this sweet strain in moving accents speak.
Ah me ! thy closing words, how deep they dwell—
" Such is thine own dear mother—guard her well."
And did I guard her, I, thy careless son ?
O Heaven, the world of duties left undone !
The chill dark grave that closes over men
Hath taught me many things I knew not then.
Scarcely remains a memory within,
But, weighed and sifted, it reveals a sin.

Better by far it seemed to me, when first
I knew hope darkened and my life reversed,

And, rudely snatched from wondering unbelief,

Saw, front to front, that ghastliness of grief,—

Better by far it seemed, a thing worth choice,

A God-sent gift, a reason to rejoice,

If I had lost thee in my tender years,

When grief, though keen, is charmed to rest by tears,

And through the world, thenceforth, our souls retain

Enough to soften, not enough to pain ;

Since no remorse for hard things done or said

Mars the remembrance of a parent dead.

For, later on, dark records graven deep

Add their own anguish to the loss we weep ;

And a misused or ineffectual Past

Claims a severe repentance to the last.

Follies we held in no account before,

Seen in their meaning pierce us to the core.

Neglected sympathies of mutual prayer,

Words left unsaid that might have soothed a care,

The light acceptance, in some heedless hour,

Of tokens heavy with affection's power,

And all the coldnesses that mar our youth,

Rise in the stern investiture of truth,

And haunt us with a load of vain regret—
God may forgive, we never can forget.
Surely, I thought, too late, or far too soon,
Heaven hath reclaimed the unutterable boon.
Just when I seemed to feel, to comprehend,
And in life's mysteries to discern an end ;
Just when my long-reluctant heart began
Some faint yet genuine recompense to plan ;
Just when I learned to understand thy worth,
Thou, my one care, wast taken from the earth.
So, mid the wreck of visions overthrown,
Robbed of my former self, I stand alone.
Inly I gaze upon the saddening scene
Of that which is, and that which might have been,
And in my spirit hoard a life-long grief,
To all unenviable—of mourners chief ;
Doomed to grow old, and fall beneath the sun,
In dire deliberation self-undone.

Better by far it seemeth to me now
In meek submission unreserved to bow,
Thanking the love that left thee here so long,
Nor joined thee earlier to that purer throng.

I would not change my wretchedness to-day

For all that earth can give or take away.

No cold philosophy can unteach this—

More pain is more capacity for bliss.

Never had any labour, any art,

Fathomed the meaning of a mother's heart,

Had not my life, through many a troubled scene,

Felt what the absence of that heart can mean.

Scarce could a gentler loss my spirit bring

To trace love-yearnings in a little thing,

And how affection moveth as she may

In each sweet office of a common day,

How through weak tasks heroic actions shine,

And one brief clause makes drudgery divine.*

All this, and more, that once seemed idle breath,

Came with conviction from the couch of death.

So, amid all the complex web of chains

Earth round me weaves, thy influence yet remains ;

So have I learned to love thee more and more ;

So have I known thee closer than before ;

So can I half rejoice thy race is run,

Since every moment makes me more thy son ;

* Herbert.

So may I meet thee, in the home on high,
Ten thousand-fold a mother when I die!

—And if of absence I could speak, forgive.
The phrase not lower than the lips doth live.
Not now the courses of my mind afar
Roam in uneasy doubt from star to star,
And wildly question earth and wandering wave
If all indeed be ended in the grave.
In calm, in pain, in waking, and in sleep,
All day, all night, I feel thy presence deep.
More than the life I breathe art thou to me,
Though unbeheld by gross mortality.
For all the fetters of his iciest charm,
Only the tangible might Death disarm.
That spirit which, even in terrestrial flight,
Was strange and admirable and infinite,
Is it not now the same, yet mightier still,
Free to go out and to return at will?
Is freedom blind of memory above?
Or shall the free remember, and not love;
Or, loving, smile in absence evermore,
Coldly debarred from all they felt before?

For me, I doubt not, though no human eye
Pierces that interval of mystery,
Lying in cloud, with dark conjectures rife,
Beyond the gates of that which we call life,
That still the dead behold me night and day,
Still hear my words, and, watching in my way,
Smile, if my deeds have worth and single scope,
Full of high sympathy and God-like hope,
True hope, not now akin to doubt and fear—
While daily I draw nearer and more near.

Limnèd upon the heart in lines more true,
More moving sweet, than ever pencil drew,
Still will I cherish thee from youth to age,
Dearest companion of my pilgrimage.
Pleasant it is to trace each well-known scene,
Musing in silence where thy feet have been,
And to be able, when my soul is drear,
To feel " A mother's lips have spoken here ;
Here the flower withers, and the leaf falls dead,
But that dear speech can never be unsaid."
Nor only thus—but every room hath grown
Impregnate with a memory of its own.

Here, kneeling with clasped hands about her chair,
We murmured lispingly our childish prayer;
Here anger died before her accents mild,
And brother was to brother reconciled;
Or kind rebuke, urged lovingly apart,
Drew generous tears, and changed the weeper's heart;
Here, worn with watchings, anxious and alone,
She calmed her sick one's suffering with her own.
Soother of pain, wherever pain might be,
Not for me only, but the most for me.

Often, a subtil anguish to assuage,
I turn, for thought, to some poetic page;
But from the first blank leaf before me rise
These words, "A mother's gift," and dim my eyes:
Three little words—yet meaning vast they bear,
Owned by my heart the sweetest poem there.
Writ with a tale whose sameness cannot pall,
That one blank leaf is more divine than all;
Yet all in their degree the charm partake,
And lofty verse grows loftier for her sake.
So, while I feed upon each hidden theme,
And link each spot with its peculiar dream,

From my rapt being falls off the crust defiled,
And once again I am a little child.
Henceforth, though good desires in frailty melt,
I cannot wholly lose what I have felt.
There lives, though planted in a barren place,
A love which is the hate of all things base.
Deeds foully done, my mother, which should be
A barrier built between my soul and thee,
Come laden with such agonies intense,
And fettered with so dire a consequence,
That still I cannot do them, if I would—
One hope preserves me negatively good.
O may I more and more that hope enfold,
Who the true substance lightly held of old !
Though in my breast there beats a wavering will
I feel that I have power to please thee still ;
And Christ, in mercy to my soul, with thine
Hath made his own pure service to combine.
I do for Him whate'er is done for thee—
How vast a boon to frail humanity !

Hence, by a road not wholly without flowers,
Cometh unnameable the hour of hours,

Rich with all wealth to which our hopes aspire,

Acmè of all experience, all desire,

When faithful eyes that hunger for the light

Feel all the wonders of God's world in sight.

Eye hath not seen, ear heard, nor spirit known,

What there the Lord will offer to His own.

Yet certain is it that no doubts or fears

Thither ascend, no partings and no tears.

Then may I see the Highest face to face!

Then may I know thee in thine own true place!

There with changed lips may I thy kindness bless!

And thine no longer shall be answerless.

L'ENVOI.

In sorrow old, but young in years,
 I would not vex life's happier round.
I envy none, I ask no tears,
 But till my own appointed ground.

Yet, if I seem to speak of grief,
 'Tis scarce worth wonder. I have known
Large losses dealt in moments brief,
 Wide harvests ere their autumn strown.

Shall I for this indulge complaint,
 Turn traitor, and cry shame on life?
No!—be my prayer, however faint,
 " Lord, help me to strive out my strife."

Though of past years I am bereft,
   Heavy with sins not hard to scan;
Yet, for the remnant that is left,
   I'll bear me as becomes a man.

And if to see another's loss
   Can make one soul aware of gain,
Come hither, and behold my cross,
   Thou who canst feel a brother's pain.

Life truly is a gorgeous dream;
   But, when the heart can understand,
Not quite so darksome as they seem
   The death-clouds loom on yonder strand.

TRANSLATIONS

HECTOR AND ANDROMACHE.

(HOMER'S ILIAD, VI. 390.)

So from the house went Hector back with speed,
Through the wide city, to the western gates,
Meaning that way to pass forth to the field.
There running, when he came, behold his wife,
Andromache, the brave Eëtion's child,
Cilician ruler, who in Thebè dwelt,
Under the woods of Placus.   With her came
A maiden, bearing on her breast the child,
Tender of soul, as yet a babe in arms,
Hector's one darling, like a lovely star.
He then beholding smiled upon his babe
In silence ; but his wife stood weeping by,
And clasped him by the hand, and spake, and said :

K

Dear one, thine own brave soul shall be thy fate.
Thou hast no pity for thy child, or me,
Ere long thy widow, when the Achaian men
Close round thee like a flood, and lay thee low—
And thou lost, I were better in my grave !
No comfort then—but sorrow.   I have now
No father, and no mother; for divine
Achilleus slew my father, when he sacked
High-gated Thebè, fair Cilician town.
Eëtion he slew there, but stripped him not ;
Awe was upon him ; with his gilded arms
He burned him, piling o'er his bones a mound ;
And elms were planted by the Oread nymphs,
Children of Zeus.   And brethren I had seven.
All in one day went down into the earth ;
Swift-foot divine Achilleus slew them all,
Mid their slow kine and sheep of silver fleece.
And for the queen my mother, with the spoil
Brought hither, whom for ransom he let go,
Her the divine maid-archer Artemis
Pierced with an arrow in her father's halls.
O Hector, thou to me art mother dear

And father, brother, husband, all in one !

Have pity, pass not from the walls, I pray,

Nor leave thy child an orphan, and thy wife

A widow.   Range beside the fig-tree hill

Thy bands, where most the city is scaleable,

And on the wall the footing easiest proved.

For by that way their bravest made assault

Thrice, with the two Aiantes, the renowned

Idomeneus, the Atridae, and the son

Of Tydeus, whether by a seer advised,

Or by their own heart evermore led on.

And the large white-plumed Hector answering

    spake :

All this I know, dear wife, and feel it all.

Yet am I filled with overpowering shame

Of long-robed Trojan women and Trojan men,

If like a dastard from the field I slink.

No, for my soul I cannot.   I have learned

Still to go forth amid the first in fight,

Building my father's glory and my own :

Albeit I know well, both in mind and heart,

That the day comes when sacred Troy shall fall,
And Priam, and his people, and his power.
Yet not the Trojan sorrow of that time,
Not Hecuba's own sorrow, nor my sire's,
Nor of my brothers, who so many and brave,
Trod by the feet of foemen, in the dust
Shall then lie mute, can touch my heart so near
As thine, when some one of the Achaian men
Leads thee bereft of freedom, in thy tears,
To Argos; there, it may be, at a loom
Not thine to work, or from Messeis well,
Or Hypereia, to bear pails in grief,
Reluctant much, yet conquered by strong fate.
Then some one may behold thy tears, and say:
' See now, the wife of Hector, first in arms,
Troy's great horse-captain in the Ilian siege.'
So will he speak, and thou shalt wail anew
For anguish, and sore need of one like me
To ward the yoke of thraldom from thy neck.
But let me lie dead in the mounded earth
Ere of thy capture and sad cries I hear!

He spake, and to the babe reached forth his arms.
Who to the bosom of his fair-zoned nurse
Clung with a cry, scared at his father's look,
And by the brass helm, and the horsehair plume,
Waving aloft so grimly. And they laughed,
Father and mother; and the nodding helm
He in a moment from his head removed,
And laid it shining on the earth, then kissed
Fondly, and dandled in his arms, the child,
And called on Zeus and all the gods in prayer:

Zeus, and all gods, let this my child become
Famed in the hosts of Troia, even as I,
In strength so good, and full of power to reign;
And, when he cometh from the fight, let men
Say 'A far better than his sire is here.'
And thus with gory spoils let him return
From the slain foe, and cheer his mother's heart!

He spake, and in the arms of his dear wife
Laid the fair babe, and to her fragrant breast

She clasped him, smiling through a mist of tears.
And Hector saw, and felt, and pitied her,
And with his hand caressed her, and thus said :

Dearest, afflict not overmuch thine heart.
No man at all can send me against fate
To Hades, and his hour can no man fly,
None, good or bad, that ever yet was born.
Go home, and look to thine own business there,
The distaff and the loom, and bid thy maids
Work—of the war shall men take thought, all men
Native in Troy, and I myself the most.

Thus spake brave Hector, and the crested helm
Took from the ground, and his dear wife passed home.
Raining sad tears, and turning oft to look.
Soon to the house she came, and found therein
Her maidens, and stirred sorrow in them all.
So Hector, yet alive, in his own house
They wailed, since no more could they hope in heart
Returning to behold him from the war.

LINES FROM SIMONIDES.

Nought among mortals can endure for ever;
  Well spake the Chian bard that men like leaves
Perish and pass away; but few endeavour
  To lay to heart the truth their ear receives:
Since each one for himself hath hope that springs
  Like nature in the bosoms of the strong,
And, while youth blooms with all delightful things,
  Deaf hearts dream visions that must fade ere long.
For none believeth in old age or death,
  Health on the sick couch turns a careless eye;
Fools, that their heart is hardened, when a breath
  Blights all their bloom, and in an hour they die:
But thou remember this, and to life's goal
Draw from the good to satisfy thy soul.

CORNELIA.

(PROPERTIUS, V. 11.)

AND now I leave thee, as a sacred trust,
That common pledge, our children ; for this care,
Branded into my dust, yet breathes and lives.
Hereafter thou, their father, take for them
A mother's office ; for thy neck must bear
The load of all my loved ones.   When thou givest
Thy kisses as they weep, add too their mother's.
Thine is the burden of the household now.
If thou have sorrow, let them see thee not ;
Beguile them, when they come, with tearless cheeks
And fond caresses.   Be it enough for thee
To weary the long nights with thoughts of me,
And the beholding of my form in dreams.

So, when thou speakest to my secret shade,

Think thou hast answer to thine every word.

But now, whether it be the door I knew

Open upon an altered wedding-couch,

And a step-mother sit where I sat once,

Speak well, my children, of your father's wife,

And bear her yoke : before your winning ways

It must be that her charmèd heart will yield.

Also praise not your mother overmuch,

For your new parent, matched with her of old,

Will think scorn of your free and innocent speech—

Or if my shade content him, and he think

My ashes of such price, learn well to mark

The coming of old age, and leave no room

For cares to enter which beset the life

Of single men.   The number of the years

Which I have lost, Heaven add unto your days !

And so may Paullus, with my offspring left,

Love to be old !   And it is well—for never

Clothed I myself in mourning for a child.

None, none was absent from my funeral rites.

But I have said.   Plead for me, ye that weep,

While grateful Earth pays back the price of life.
Yea, heaven itself hath opened to the good.
And may my bones, for all that I have wrought.
Ride on triumphant to the fields of rest!

LINES FROM OVID.

(TRISTIA, V. 12.)

"STUDY the mournful hours away,
    Lest in dull sloth thy spirit pine."
Hard words thou writest : verse is gay,
    And asks a lighter heart than mine.

No calms my stormy life beguile,
    Than mine can be no sadder chance ;
You bid bereavèd Priam smile,
    And Niobe, the childless, dance.

Is grief or study more my part,
    Whose life is doomed to wilds like these ?
Though you should make my feeble heart
    Strong with the strength of Socrates,

Such ruin would crush wisdom down ;
   Stronger than man is wrath divine.
That sage, whom Phœbus gave the crown,
   Never could write in grief like mine.

Can I my land and thee forget,
   Nor the felt sorrow wound my breast ?
Say that I can—but foes beset
   This place, and rob me of all rest.

Add that my mind hath rusted now,
   And fallen far from what it was.
The land, though rich, that lacks the plough
   Is barren, save of thorns and grass.

The horse, that long hath idle stood,
   Is soon o'ertaken in the race ;
And, torn from its familiar flood,
   The chinky pinnace rots apace.

Nor hope that I, before but mean,
   Can to my former self return ;

Long sense of ills hath bruised my brain,
    Half the old fires no longer burn.

Yet oft I take the pen, and try,
    As now, to build the measured rhyme.
Words come not, or, as meet thine eye,
    Words worthy of their place and time.

Last, glory cheers the heart that fails,
    And love of praise inspires the mind—
I followed once Fame's star, my sails
    Filled with a favourable wind.

But now 'tis not so well with me,
    To care if fame be lost or won.
Nay, but I would, if that might be,
    Live all unknown beneath the sun.

FRAGMENT FROM OVID.

No day so damp with the mist and cloud,
  That the rains never cease in the air ;
No place so rude with the brambly wood
  But some useful herb groweth there ;
And nothing by Fate is so desolate
  But a smile may be found somewhere.

EPIGRAM BY PLATO.

In rapture on the stars above
Thou gazest, O my star, my love.
Would that I were those happy skies,
To see thee with ten thousand eyes !

THE RECANTATION.

(HORACE, OD. I. 16.)

LOVELY mother's lovelier daughter,
 Those sharp verses, edged with blame,
Hurl into the Adrian water,
 Cancel, if thou wilt, with flame.
Rhea from her mountain-hollow,
 Liber at his royal feasts,
From his Delphian shrine Apollo,
 Shake the spirit of their priests.
Hark! the votaries loud and often
 Shrilly clanging cymbals ring—
These are savage, but may soften—
 Anger is a sterner thing.
Not the ship-destroying ocean,
 Noric steel, or flaming fire,

Not the storm-god's mighty motion,
　　Fright it from its purpose dire.
When Prometheus first transmuted
　　Atoms culled for human clay,
Deep the lion's rage he rooted
　　In our breast, as legends say.
Anger with a grievous ruin
　　Smote Thyestes and his line ;
This, the fount of sheer undoing,
　　Left of cities scarce a sign,
When, among the sworded nations,
　　Armies flushed with pride and spoil
Ploughed up many a state's foundations
　　Planted in imperial soil.
Curb thy soul with juster measures—
　　Me youth's sweetness, prone to wrong,
Heated into quick displeasures,
　　And an ill-directed song.
Now my bitterness would mellow ;
　　I annul the trenchant strain ;
Be once more my true love-fellow ;
　　Take me to thy heart again !

THE MEAN.

(HORACE, OD. II. 10.)

THIS is the better life, dear friend,
Not always in mid sea to wend,
Nor yet distrustfully portend
      Storms hourly near,
And hug, not wisely in the end,
      Ill shores in fear.

That man who in his soul hath seen
How lovely is the golden mean,
He lacks the wretchedness unclean
      Of used-up walls ;
He lacks, in soberness serene,
      Wealth's envied halls.

Pines of a stature proud and vast
Shake oftener when the winds rush past,
Down to the earth high towers are cast
  With heavier fall,
And still the fiery lightnings blast
  The hill-tops tall.

The breast, that wisdom's rule obeys,
Hopes for a change in evil days,
And fears it amid prosperous ways
  Remote from ill ;
Since God both causes and allays
  Our storms at will.

If fortune fail thee now, yet know
It will not evermore be so ;
Apollo may his lute forego,
  But not for ever,
Nor bears he always a strung bow
  And armèd quiver.

Thou, when adversities ensue,

Prove thyself constant, brave, and true,

And, when the risks seem far and few,

    Mid favouring gales

Furl in good hour, with caution due,

    Thy swelling sails.

LOVE RENEWED.

(HORACE, OD. III. 9.)

HORACE.

WHILE to thee no other name was nearer,
    Ere a rival youth aspired to fling
Round thy snow-white neck embraces dearer,
    I lived richer than a Persian king.

LYDIA.

Ere a new flame to thy false heart beckoned,
    When the elder passion seemed divine,
Nor was Lydia yet to Chloë second,
    Roman Ilia's glory paled to mine.

HORACE.

Now lute-learnèd, skilled in measures tender,
    Thracian Chloë doth my heart enslave.

Life for her I dread not to surrender,
If the fates my other soul will save.

LYDIA.

Child of Thurian Ornytus I cherish ;
Mutual flames to me doth Calaïs bear.
Twice for him will I consent to perish,
If the fates my darling boy will spare.

HORACE.

What if yet the ancient love returning
Re-unite in brazen yoke us twain,
If this door, the gold-haired Chloë spurning,
Welcome cast-off Lydia once again ?

LYDIA.

He is fairer than a star in heaven,
Thou more fierce than Adria's restive sea,
Light as cork—yet oh ! since choice is given,
Let me live and love and die with thee !

CIVIL WAR.

(Horace, Epod. 7.)

Whither, O whither rush ye in fell wrath?
 Why fit the sheathèd sword to red right hands?
Too little hath there yet of Latian death
 Crimsoned the seas and lands?

Not that the envious Punic citadel
 Should fall in fire on Rome's victorious day,
Or the chained Briton, once invincible,
 Move down the Sacred Way.

But that thou mayest the Parthian prayer fulfil,
 A self-destroying city. Not such mind
Have wolves or lions, such a thirst to kill;
 They war not with their kind.

Doth some blind fury, or a spur more keen,

   Urge you, or crime? I pray you, let me know.

None answers—their pale stupor may be seen:

   Their stricken blood beats low.

This is it: evil bitter fates impel

   Rome's children, the fraternal murder's crime,

Our deep inheritance, since Remus fell,

   Of curse unto all time.

HECTOR'S FAREWELL.

(SCHILLER.)

ANDROMACHE.

Will my Hector thus depart for ever
Where Achilles' wrathful hands deliver
  To his slain Patroclus offerings dread?
Where in spear-craft is thy children's teacher,
Where of honour to the gods the preacher,
  When abysmal Orcus holds thee dead?

HECTOR.

Dearest wife, refrain thy voice of mourning,
For the field of fight my soul is burning,
  And these arms our Pergamus must save.
For the gods' most holy hearth contending,
And the homes of fatherland defending,
  Pass I downward to the Stygian wave.

ANDROMACHE.

Nevermore, alas ! thine armour clangeth ;
Idly in the hall thine iron hangeth ;
    Priam's heroes fall around their sire.
Thou art gone to where no day-star beameth ;
Through the glooms Cocytus moaning streameth ;
    E'en thy love in Lethe will expire.

HECTOR.

Let each feeling, hope, and thought I cherish,
In the silent-rolling Lethe perish !
    Only Love shall never die.
Hark ! the war-cry on the walls is sounding ;
Gird my sword upon me ; cease desponding ;
    Hector's love in Lethe cannot die !

LOYAL DEATH.

(Körner.)

The knight must forth unto the field of blood,
　Freedom, Fame, Fatherland, his banner's token :
But first before his loved one's home he stood ;
　He could not leave that fond farewell unspoken.
　　　" Let not weak tears thine eyes bedew ;
　　　　Hope lives in earth, and help above ;
　　　And Death shall ever find me true,
　　　　True to my Fatherland and Love."

Thus spake he the last words he came to bring,
　Then to the loyal host his good steed bore him :
He hastened to the standards of his king,
　And fearless eyed the gathering foe before him.

" I reck not of yon clouds of death.

Though hence I nevermore remove,

Joyfully will I yield my breath,

Fighting for Fatherland and Love."

Then where the fire was fiercest on he rode ;

His path was marked by thousands dead and dying.

Men to his hero-arm the victory owed ;

But with the vanquished was the victor lying—

" Stream on, my blood, flow redly now ;

My sword doth thy avenger prove.

True to the last I kept my vow,

And died for Fatherland and Love."

TRANSLATIONS OF SACRED PIECES

DIES IRÆ.

(THOMAS OF CELANO.—About A.D. 1230.)

DAY of anger, day of wonder,
When the world shall roll asunder.
Quenched in fire and smoke and thunder !

O vast terror, wild heart-rending,
Of that hour when Earth is ending,
And her jealous Judge descending ;

When the trumpet's voice astoundeth,
Through earth's sepulchres reboundeth,
Summons universal soundeth !

Death astonied, Nature shaken,
Sees all creatures, as they waken,
To that dire tribunal taken.

Lo ! the Book, where all is hoarded,
Not a secret unrecorded :
Every doom is thence awarded.

So the Judge, when He arraigneth,
Every hidden thing explaineth :
Nothing unavenged remaineth.

In that fiery revelation
Where shall I make supplication,
When the just hath scarce salvation ?

Fount of Love, dread King supernal,
Freely giving life eternal,
Save me from the pains infernal !

This forget not, sweet Life-giver,
Me Thou camest to deliver :
Cast me not away for ever !

Seeking me Thy sad life lasted,

On the cross death's pains were tasted ;

Let not toil like this be wasted !

God of righteous retribution,

Grant my sins full absolution

Ere Thy wrath's last execution !

Lo, I stand with face suffusèd,

Groaning, in my guilt accusèd ;

Spare my soul, with sorrow bruisèd !

By the Magdalene forgiven,

By the dying robber shriven,

I too cherish hope of heaven.

Though my prayers are full of failing,

Save me, of Thy grace availing,

From the pit of endless wailing !

M

On Thy right a place provide me,
With Thy chosen sheep beside me :
From the goats, good Lord, divide me !

When to penal fire are driven
Those who would not be forgiven,
Call me with Thy saints to heaven !

Kneeling, crushed in heart, before Thee,
Sad and suppliant I adore Thee :
Hear me, save me, I implore Thee !

STABAT MATER.

(GIACOPONE.—Died A.D. 1306.)

STOOD the maiden Mother weeping,
By the Cross her sad watch keeping,
  Near her dying Son and Lord ;
Woes wherewith the heart is broken,
Sorrows never to be spoken,
  Smote her, pierced her like a sword.

O with what vast griefs oppressèd
Bowed the more than woman blessèd,
  Mother of God's only Son !
O what bitterness came o'er her,
When the dread doom passed before her,
  Seeing her Beloved undone !

Say, can any stand by tearless,
When so woe-begone and cheerless
   Mourns the Virgin undefiled,
Or the rising anguish smother,
When he sees the tenderest mother
   Suffer with her suffering Child?

Sacrifice for sins presented,
Jesus she beheld tormented,
   For her people scourged and slain;
In His hour of desolation,
In the spirit's separation,
   She beheld her dear one's pain.

Love's pure fountain, let me borrow
From thine anguish sense of sorrow;
   Make me, Mother, mourn with thee :
Be my heart's best offerings given
Evermore to Christ in heaven;
   Let me His true servant be !

Holy Mother, draw me, win me,
Plant the Crucified within me,
    Brand His wounds upon my heart !
For my sake thy Child was stricken !
With His blood my spirit quicken ;
    Half His agonies impart !

Let me feel thy sore affliction,
And my Master's crucifixion
    Share, till life's last dawn appears ;
So, with thee His cross frequenting,
Daily would I kneel repenting,
    Meek companion of thy tears.

Virgin-queen, renowned for ever,
Not from me thy sweetness sever ;
    Bid me drink thy sorrow's cup,
Till my sympathizing spirit
All Christ's bitter pangs inherit,
    All His bleeding wounds count up.

Pierce me with my Saviour's piercings,
Let me taste the cross and cursings,
   And for love the wine-press tread !
Through thy kindling inspiration,
Virgin, let me find salvation
   In the doom of quick and dead !

Let Christ's guardian cross attend me,
And His saving death defend me,
   Cradled in His arms of love !
When the body sleeps forsaken,
Mother, let my soul awaken
   In God's Paradise above !

THE PASSION.

(BONAVENTURA.—Died A.D. 1274.)

O WHAT shame and desolation,
Working out the world's salvation,
 Deigned the King of Heaven to bear!
See Him, bowed with sorrows endless,
Hungry, thirsty, poor, and friendless,
 Even to the cross repair!

Hold His wrongs in recollection,
Who, in undeserved affliction,
 Wandered through a thankless land :
Countless agonies unmeasured
In thy heart of hearts keep treasured,
 If at all thou understand.

To the cross from judgment taken,
Silent, of His friends forsaken,
From no torments doth He shrink ;
There His hands and feet they piercèd,
There of gall, as one accursèd,
Gave the King of kings to drink !

See, the eye no longer flashes,
And the face is white like ashes—
Furrowed with an iron pain.
On that blessèd form unshrouded
Ancient comeliness is clouded ;
Scarce doth any grace remain.

Whoso hearest and believest,
See that in this grief thou grievest;
Groan for heaviness of heart ;
Vex thy flesh, thy soul, with sorrow ;
Weeping reach thy hand, and borrow
From the cross each cruel smart.

With the curse upon Him lying,

Mark the Man of sorrows dying,

 Strong in pain, our crowning Seed—

Justly, then, be thou contented

With thy Lord to be tormented,

 On the cross with Him to bleed.

Brother, in all work whatever

Still to see Christ's wounds endeavour,

 Still take up the cross He bore ;

Count Him thine eternal treasure,

Let thine heart, with deepening pleasure,

 Feed upon Him more and more.

Crucified, sustain Thy servant,

Make my soul with anguish fervent

 Feel Thy passion day by day.

Lovingly I yearn to cherish

That sweet cross where Thou didst perish,

 In Thine arms to pass away !

ST ANDREW TO THE CROSS.

(BEDE.—Died A.D. 735.)

HAIL victory's most sacred sign,
  Hail glorious monument of grace,
Cross, on whose breast the Lord divine
  Died to redeem our fallen race !

How glorious and how strong to save
  Gleam far and wide thy virtues rare,
Hallowed by Christ Himself, who gave
  To thee His reverend limbs to bear !

Of old around thee, sore-distrest,
  Crouched the pale habitants of earth,

Who now in the believing breast
    Dost plant love's sanctifying mirth.

This is faith's pastime—when thine arms
    In rest a sainted form enfold,
While (crown of all thy gracious charms)
    He sees the gates of heaven unrolled.

The sweet limbs of our Saviour make
    Thy wood than honey sweeter far.
We count thee worthy for His sake,
    Yea better than all things that are.

Now gladly at thy foot I stand ;
    I clasp thee round with arms of love ;
And to thee clinging, heart and hand,
    Climb to the blessedness above.

Kind one, take up the humblest slave
    Of Him who on thy glorious tree,
My Lord and Master, freely gave
    The treasures of His life for me.

Thus Andrew spake, when he beheld
The Cross set for his final strife—
Then to the soldier standing by
His garment gave, and, lifted high,
Slept on the tree of life.

THE RESURRECTION.

(PETER THE VENERABLE. --Died A.D. 1156.)

MAGDALENE, thy grief lay down,
 Calm thine eyelids' tearful shower !
'Tis no longer Simon's feast,
 'Tis no longer sorrow's hour.
Thousand blisses round thee spring ;
These thy soul are summoning.
　　　Hallelujah !

Magdalene, thy smile take up,
 Stamp with mirth thy lucid brow !
Punishment and pain are fled,
 Light is shining o'er thee now.
Jesus Christ hath freed the world,
And strong Death to ruin hurled.
　　　Hallelujah !

Magdalene, aloud rejoice !
 Christ returneth from the grave.
All the agony is past ;
 Death the king is Death the slave.
He whom dying thou didst weep
Wakes triumphant from His sleep.
   Hallelujah !

Magdalene, thine eyes lift up,
 View thy Lord with mute amaze !
Mark the merciful sweet brow,
 On the five wounds wondering gaze,
Which like pearls about Him shine,
Decking the new Life Divine.
   Hallelujah !

Magdalene, take life and live !
 For thy light hath risen again.
Now behold, with leaping heart,
 Blotted out Death's power of pain.
Sunless sorrow far hath flown ;
Make the songs of Love thine own.
   Hallelujah !

EASTER HYMN.

(ADAM OF ST VICTOR.—Died about A.D. 1180.)

WELCOME the triumphal token,
   Day to ruined world how sweet !
When the foeman's power was broken,
   And our ills found comfort meet.
Know ye not this day so splendid,
   Shining with so fair a crown,
Witnessed sin's dominion ended,
   And the Evil One cast down ?

Then, the Prince of darkness flying,
   Every baneful charm did cease,
Health came to the sick and dying,
   Rose on earth the reign of peace ;

Death the sting of death undoing,
    Hope of life returned to-day ;
Sin's stronghold was hurled to ruin,
    And pollution chased away.

Since then Christ our souls hath cherished
    In a union such as this,
And on earth hath freely perished
    For the things we wrought amiss,
Rightly may we hymn His story,
    And our paschal banquet spread,
Heart, word, work proclaim His glory,
    Rising with Him from the dead !

HYMN TO THE HOLY SPIRIT.

(ROBERT II. OF FRANCE.—Died A.D. 1031.)

Come, O Holy Spirit, come ;
Earthward from Thy heavenly home
Flash the flowing radiance bright.

Come, Thou Father of the poor ;
Come, Thou Giver of good store ;
Come, of hearts Thou sovran light.

Comforter the truest, best,
Who the soul with pleasant rest
Pleasantly dost entertain :

Ease in toil and cordial sweet,
Shelter in the burning heat,
Soothing influence in pain.

N

O most blessed blessed Light,
Shine with splendour pure and white.
Shine upon Thy saints within ;

For in man, without Thy grace,
Nothing ever can have place,
Nothing void of shame and sin.

Wash to whiteness every stain,
Slake the thirsty soil with rain,
Heal the hurt that needs Thy care ;

Bend the stubborn to Thy sway,
Cheer the cold with genial day,
Make the crooked straight and clear.

Holy Spirit, to the just,
Who in Thee believe and trust,
Give the sacred Sabbath-rest ;

Give the guerdon they have won,
Give supreme salvation's crown,
Give the ages ever blest.

TO THE HOLY SPIRIT.

(Adam of St Victor.)

Thou from Father, Son, proceeding,
Sanctify our praise and pleading,
 Paraclete, enthroned above—
Lips of inspiration lend us,
And responsive ardours send us
 To Thine own rich flames of love.

Hail by Father, Son, belovèd !
Equal unto each, approvèd
 Peer of perfect Deity;
All things filling, all sustaining,
Warder of the stars, and reigning
 Moveless o'er the moving sky.

Light the clearest, Light the dearest,
Who our inward darkness cheerest
    With Thy cloud-dissolving ray.
By Thine advent men are mended,
Sin departs, her empire ended,
    And sin's rust is wiped away.

Knowledge of the truth Thou sowest;
Thou the road of justice showest,
    And the pleasant paths of peace.
Far from hearts perverse Thou fliest,
But, where goodness is, suppliest
    Access to Thy mysteries.

Nothing dark where Thou explainest;
Nothing foul where Thou remainest;
    Thy pervading presence bright
Wakes exultant spirit-voices;
Conscience feelingly rejoices
    In the cleanness of Thy light.

Thou canst render heart-strings tender,
And expellest, where Thou dwellest,
    Clouds of heaviness and gloom.
Flaming ever, burning never,
Hallowed fires from pain deliver
    Human souls, where Thou dost come.

Intellects that erewhile slumbered,
With a deadening crust encumbered,
    Quicken in Thy glorious light.
Into speech-divine Thou mouldest
Tongues, and lovingly upholdest
    Hearts made ready for the right.

Help of souls for succour groaning,
Comforter of mourners moaning,
    Refuge of the friendless poor,
Teach us to cast off the leaven
Of this earth : to Thine own Heaven
    Every erring love restore ;
Clear from taint what wrong hath blighted,
Reconcile the disunited,
    Be our safeguard evermore !

Thou who once, in visitation,
Strength and lofty consolation
　　To Thy trembling Church didst send,
Visit, if it be Thy pleasure,
Even *us*, and in like measure
　　All who at Thine altars bend.

Equal majesty and power
Stand the everlasting dower
　　Of the Godhead—Three in One.
Thou, the Third, art rightly reckoned
Equal with the First and Second;
　　Ordered scale existeth none.

Wherefore, in Thy mighty Presence,
Sharer of the Father's essence,
　　Humbly do Thy servants sue.
We to God the Father ever
And to God the Son deliver
　　And to Thee our praises due.

MAN.

(Alanus.—Died about a.d. 1200.)

Like a picture all creation
Standeth for our contemplation,
   'Tis our mirror and our book.
Life and death are there presented,
All our pilgrimage imprinted,
   Calling men to pause and look.

For the rose doth paint our story,
And the rose doth glass our glory,
   Readeth all our life's brief hour.
In the early morn she bloometh;
Agèd, when the evening gloometh,
   Falls off the deflowered flower.

Breathing she her life exhaleth ;
Soon her blushing beauty paleth ;
   Dying came the flower to earth ;
Old and new, alike death-laden,
Agèd, yet a youthful maiden,
   Fading in her dawn of birth.

So unto the youthful comer
Ministers his mortal summer ;
   Brightly smiles the fleeting flower—
But that morning hath its even,
Soon athwart the darkling heaven
   Cometh on life's twilight hour.

Pain is all man's life and being,
Toil without a hope of fleeing ;
   Death descending covers all.
Sunshine now is storm hereafter ;
Death tracks life, and sorrow laughter ;
   Darkness on our day doth fall.

Therefore, when this clause thou readest,
See that thou the lesson heedest;
    Man, thy life is figured clear;
In what state thou camest hither,
What to-day thou art, and whither
    Tend thy steps, examine here.

Weep the cost of past transgression,
Wail thy sin, tame pride and passion,
    Cast thy haughtiness away;
Reinsman of the mind and master,
Guard thy trust, lest foul disaster
    Find thee unawares astray.

LOVE IN DEATH.

Hearken and heed my call,
Zion's true daughters all ;
Pity me, faint and sick,
Tell ye my true love quick :—
Wounded of love I lie,
Wounded of love I die !

Slow creep the languid hours ;
Pillow my head with flowers ;
With fairest fruit of gold
Pray you my form enfold ;
Fire that no tears can stay
Eateth my heart away !

Sisters, with haste prepare
Woods of all odours rare,

Breathing the boon of sleep :
Pile them up broad and deep.
Mine be that Phœnix-pyre !
Thence will I mount in fire !

Whether love pain may prove,
Whether pain be but love,
I have no skill to tell—
This only know I well ;
If pain but love may be,
Pain seemeth sweet to me.

When will thy torments cease ?
Hence with reprieve or peace !
Break this slow agony ;
Moments are years to me :
Death-pains so lingering,
Ah, love ! thy wounds do bring !

Break, Spirit, break thy chain,
Sunder life's cords in twain !

Lo, to the halls sublime

Yearns the pure flame to climb!

Heaven in my view doth stand :

There is my fatherland!

THE DAY OF DEATH.

(Peter Damiani.—Died a.d. 1072.)

Heavily with dread thou loomest, last day of my
earthly life ;

Heart and melting reins within me shudder at the
mortal strife,

When I would inform my spirit with what horrors
thou art rife !

Who can dare the scene discover that doth compass
thee about,

When the feeble flesh uncoileth, and life's span is
measured out,

And the soul reluctant rushes on the mystery without ?

Sense is dead, the dry tongue stiffens, and the eyes
　　grow dim for death,
And the sick man's breast is heaving, and his hoarse
　　throat gasps for breath,
Blanched his cheeks, his limbs hang nerveless, and his
　　beauty vanisheth.

Things he wrought, and thought, and uttered, in the
　　years he lived below,
Rob him of his rest ; dread visions round his couch of
　　anguish grow,
Come up from the Past and daunt him, hunt his
　　glances to and fro.

Then the thought of ended action doth his lonely
　　spirit sting ;
Then his conscience racks him ever with untimely
　　visiting ;
But his terrible repentance cometh now a fruitless
　　thing.

In that hour are very bitter all the sweetnesses of
earth,
When the endless retribution tracks the footsteps of
his mirth;
All that once was grand and glorious seemeth to him
nothing-worth.

Christ, Invincible, I pray Thee help me; Lord, respect
my moan;
When the last dark hour is on me and I journey
hence alone,
Suffer not the powers of evil then to claim me for
their own.

Slay in me the Prince of darkness; let hell fall Thy
grace before!
Thy lost sheep, redeemed for ever, then unto Thy fold
restore,
There to dwell in contemplation of Thy glory evermore.

PRINTED BY WILLIAM BLACKWOOD AND SONS, EDINBURGH.